Lisa Samson weaves a luminous tapestry of a father's love for his son in a story so pure it makes your heart lowing for more. The vibrant hues of life in all its fullness, from simple pleasures to unforeseen trials, artfully entwine with the profound wisdom of a man whose salutary truths cannot be denied. When the narrative comes full circle, we see a masterpiece – an intricate design of what could be if each of us humbly gave and received love, grace, and mercy without any judgements to veil their brilliant light. Literary fiction at its finest!

    —SUSAN MIURA, award-winning author of the Healer series and Surviving Carmelita

"I've been reading Lisa Samson's books for nearly two decades, and this is what I know for sure: the person I am when I turn the first page, will have laughed, cried, been broken open, healed, put back together again, and astonished by the time I close the book. Her work is nothing short of transformative. Read it if you want to grow wiser, more compassionate, and full of wonder for all the beauty in God's often challenging world."

    —CLAUDIA LOVE MAIR, author of Don't You Fall Now and Zora and Nicky: a Novel in Black and White.

WE HAD STARS IN OUR EYES

an uplit novel by

LISA SAMSON

The Salish Sea Press

Orcas Island, Washington

We Had Stars in Our Eyes

Kindle eBook edition ISBN: 978-1-63613-008-8
Paperback edition ISBN: 978-1-63613-007-1

Artwork and Cover design by Lisa Samson:
https://lisajoysamson.com

Interior book design by Carmen Barber:
KeepingYouWriting@gmail.com

First published in the United States June, 2021, by The Salish Sea Press, a program of SpiritVenture Ministries, Box 1492, Absecon, NJ 08201. https://salishsea.press

For Jake, who loves love.

Dear Friend,

However you came to this book, I hope you leave it feeling loved and maybe a little better equipped to love others in a way that brings joy and meaning to your life.

In the winter of 2020, just before the pandemic hit, this book flowed out of me and into a composition book. I wish I could take credit for the wisdom and active love John exhibits to his son, Taliesin, in these pages. But the truth is, I needed it more than anyone.

I debated on whether or not to hone this and release it. This is really more of a wisdom book than a novel. But it seems like a good time for it. Many fathers seek guidance and many mothers are raising children alone and could use John's words. Our lives bear their own story, and if we listen to the Spirit within us and the good people around us, our story can be changed into something which, while hard, can be filled with more direction and less internal anguish. These are my hopes for this story. And my hope for you.

Much love to you as you set out on this journey with Tally and John. Know you are loved with an everlasting love, and the Good Parent who made us all, is always ready to impart wisdom even as you gain understanding in your life experiences. You are never out of The Creator's sight and can constantly avail yourself of God's care. Just ask.

Sincerely Yours,

Lisa Samson
May 20, 2021
Louisville, Kentucky

I ARRIVED ON this planet during a glorious July according to the only meaningful account.

"I'll never forget how the sun came out and shone through the raindrops like a gathering of stars. Right at the moment the doctor said, 'Your wife had a little boy, sir.' Right there out the window behind the doctor the world lit up. And it never returned completely to what it was before. That light was added for good that day, Son."

That light was me, he would tell me.

Goodwill resounded in waves from the heart of my father who held me aloft in work-worn hands right there in the hallway of the maternity ward. He proclaimed in quite the unusual manner for the normally quiet craftsman, "Behold! The one on whom my favor rests!"

My father laughed, along with the duty nurses, a couple of orderlies, the man delivering lunches, and an older fellow on crutches in a backless gown worn frontless who called out, "Yes, sirree!" He batoned his crutch, closing the gown a few more inches from the left—much to the relief of the informal assembly gathered in the sacralized fumes of birth and disinfectant.

From there, my father spent the rest of our time on Earth together proving he meant each of those words. Though he's been gone but seven days, I am realizing anew what a beautiful human existence he gave to an ordinary human like me, and how, secure in a father's love, that same ordinary human could create a life reflecting beauty and goodness to the world.

I know this. We pass along the stars dancing in our eyes. My father did so for me, and by telling our story, I hope to do the same for others.

IN THE SPRING of 1942, my stint in the U.S. Navy sent me—and a bunch of other guys just like me who didn't know better than to volunteer for an actual war—to patrol the waters off the coast of France. I did my best to fit in, but there are some pretenses beyond one's abilities. And I knew mine. Youthful suspicions that my father differed from many other fathers forged with tales of childhood crucibles into fact. Father-stories illuminated the closely shared space like campfire tales. Negligent fathers. Absent fathers. Abusive fathers. Weak fathers. Work-addled fathers. Lazy fathers. Many sounded like middling patriarchs content to let their wives raise the kids, not really wanting to be bothered—after all, the mortgage was paid and where's the evening paper, dear?

The weaving of paternal yarns aboard ship knit three things together inside me for future reference: tragedy eventually normalized for some; true fatherhood is a privilege, it is held as sacred, and is as precious to a man as the children involved; and finally, if my perception of my shipmates was cut from whole cloth, all children are precious no matter their age or their sire. Each would have died for the other.

At sea on the Atlantic, I sat watching the sun exit stage left with little ado in a cloudless sky, drawing me toward the direction of home. I missed home. I missed our routine. I missed the daily caring my father brought, but at that very moment, I would have admitted to none of it. This longing, privately treasured, belonged solely to me.

I eventually joined the nightly group gathered around a deck of playing cards. Comparing childhood woes, each survival story coiled, ready to sink fangs into its predecessor.

Ed, a great mechanic, left home at twelve. He zigzagged his way across the country, washing dishes and hitching rides until he ended up at a garage in Kalispell. "I fold. Nobody bothered about finding me." He threw down his cards. "Not that I want anything to do with any of them jackasses."

Another boasted three broken bones. "By age seven."

Lou, a SuppO crusted over by years on salt water, scratched a non-existent beard. "When I turned seventeen, my father handed me a can of beans, a can opener, a carton of Luckies, and showed me the door."

"What about you, Tal?" asked James, a quiet man from Mississippi, still deliberating the efficacy of his hand.

"I fold, too." I laid my cards face down on the table. "Gents, my dad is near perfect. I got nothing on you boys. Carry on, though."

Brett, who tried his best in the kitchen, bless him, tossed his cards aside. "Ha! What do you expect from a corpsman anyway?"

No gun. No guts. No glory.

But I laughed with him and the rest of the gang. "Listen, you can make fun of me all you want, but when something backfires on you, I'm the one. And you know that's true."

"I would rather fire a gun than stitch live skin back together." Lou toasted me, shuddering like one asked to scoop up three-day-old roadkill with his teeth.

We all threw back the shot he poured in our water glasses.

Lou toasted anything he liked.

The game fell apart. Who won, who lost didn't really matter then—and it surely doesn't now.

Ed settled back into his chair. "So, tell us little about your father if he's so great. Personally, I could use something a little happier right about now."

At the risk of sounding like an annoying little braggart, my words poured forth as if from an invisible tumbler of sunlight down into a world birthed in shadow for many who gathered. They drank them in, the thirst raging in their eyes. They heard the truth of it, rendered for everyday use.

Soon enough, other tales unraveled and the bravado started up, its noise drowning out the sorrow.

I may have lost the game of who's-got-the-worst-story, but I never wanted to play it anyway, with anybody, about anything. My father taught me that.

"You want the worst story, Son? The world will

hop on board and make sure that happens for you. It's the darndest thing I've ever seen."

Like most of my father's words, I took them to heart.

A WEEK LATER, I required more than a little stitching back together after my left hand took a nosedive off the coast of France. The boys made sure to remind me of our backfiring conversation when they filed into the sick bay the day before I flew back to the States for surgery.

"How did you know?" asked James.

"Glad I didn't," I said.

Lou shook his head. "Weird if you ask me, you stupid son of a—"

"Way to get out of the war, Tally." Ed laughed.

Humor can be pretty dark in the armed forces, but it's a very dark business. We make ourselves find light in the strangest of places. We have to.

L IBERATED TWO MONTHS later from both Walter Reed and the open seas, I'd sacrificed enough for my country. A Navy corpsman needed both hands as much as anyone, guns or not.

It hurt like hell.

My first great loss as a young man felt like overkill if meant for a life lesson.

My father assured me character lessons don't start out that drastically. "It was an accident, Son," he wrote. "No sense in torturing yourself about it otherwise."

A man given to helping out by nature, he began carving a prosthesis at the first news of my hand's final wave goodbye. His daily letters as I recovered and rehabbed—words of hope, encouragement, and support—attached to the detritus of despair swimming like microorganisms in my depths. He kept my spirits from sinking completely, and I knew, I knew, I knew I wouldn't have to figure out alone what came next. In fact, he wrote down those very words. My father believed leaving a person guessing at the truth was its own sort of lie.

5

"If I could give you my own hand, Son, I would."

He whispered these words in my ear as soon as I had descended the train steps and into his firm embrace. Then, pulling back, he cemented a gaze between us. "Hello, Son. I'm glad you're home."

"I am, too, Dad. It's good to see you."

If I had said those words every time my eyes directly received the light continually flaming inside him, not one time would they have been untrue.

I sunk into him—for my father was a large man, and I am not—casting my sorrow onto the only person life had presented me for doing so. And hope began to form like a warm mist, my cold despair harder to see, unable to reach the marrow it craved.

6

W<small>E SETTLED IN</small> for club sandwiches at the Woolworth lunch counter two blocks from our apartment, a treat my father and I established years before on haircut Saturdays. We swiveled on chrome stools upholstered with worn, black leather, and plucked menus from the metal clip on the salt and pepper holder. A radio at the grill gave voice to the Inkspots, who gave voice to my own sentiment of not wishing to set the world on fire. I had seen enough of that sort of thing to last a lifetime.

Our much beloved waitress, a rosy-brown woman named Dominique, greeted us from the soda machine. She pulled root beer down over three scoops of vanilla ice cream. "Hello, gentlemen! The usual? And I don't know why I bother asking, other than sometimes people go against their nature for no apparent good reason."

We all laughed together. My father's second favorite sound.

"Not today, Dominique," my father said. "We're valuing tradition at all costs."

"Welcome home, Tally. Glad you made it out of that rat trap." Before I left for basic, Dominque had made quite clear her opinion about being stuck at sea no matter how large the boat. "I'd have gone crazy." She turned and presented a cherry Coke and the float to an older couple at the end of the counter.

She didn't notice my left arm, crooked and resting on my lap. My gaze searched her molten-gold eyes the entire time she attended to us. I said so to my father after the glass door closed behind us.

"I wouldn't be so sure, Son. Dominique's one of those holy people that know more than they let on."

7

THE SUBSEQUENT WALK through our neighborhood offered up live performances of everything my daydream theater produced for two months as my amputation throbbed, burned, and pretended it possessed a hand. We rounded a few corners to the spot of earth covered by a square mass of blonde brick and plate-glass windows known as Frum's Corner Store. Hand-lettered signs announcing the specials Mister Roberts gave as gifts to his neighbors cut some of the bright sun that heated up the store in unbearable measure during summer heat waves.

Mister Elmer Roberts, Frum's owner, a very short man with four children twelve and under, placated a rather flamboyant wife who favored purple and robin's-egg blue. His live-in mother, ghostly gentle, warbled parlor music to herself, two mean calicoes, one gray, shaggy canine he called "Lazy Man Jones," and three blind mice according to his humorous listing upon meeting a new customer. Squished together in the apartment over the store, the unseen family presence emitting in thumps, scratches and, "There's a long, long trail a-winding" inspired a routine most of us regulars could recite with him.

"Look what the wind blew in!" he cried from beneath his grand mustaches.

That day, be it known, Mister Roberts lifted a bottle of liquor from under the refrigerated meat case to Grandmother's rendition of *Down In the Valley*. He slanted its contents into three juice glasses.

"To homecomings!" he said.

"Homecomings!"

We all tapped our glasses on the wooden counter and threw Old No. 7 against the back of our throats. He side-handed the large totaling button on his hulking brass cash register. The ornate drawer shot out a grand underbite and the bell of sale tolled for me. He pushed in the drawer and twice repeated the process signaling to the regulars taking advantage of the daily special. *Three cans of pinto beans for the price of two.* And no, not two for the price of one, everybody. There's a war going on, in case you hadn't noticed.

Yes, he loved his neighbors, but God never expected a man to go bankrupt doing so, isn't that so, Tally?

He pulled out a tray of glasses and transferred the remaining contents of the bottle to their insides.

When all had taken their glass in hand, he held his aloft.

"Taliesin has lost his hand in the waters of the ocean, my friends. Long live Taliesin!"

So much for Dominique's offered anonymity. Not that

it felt any less holy, to be accurate.

"Long live Taliesin!" they boomed.

My father shouted louder than anybody, and we tossed back our second shot, curling our lips across our teeth in the fumed aftermath.

Glory finds herself in the strangest places, sleeping with those who recognize in her what the pious fail to see. Unless they're looking for beans on special. A good deal wields its own glory, to be certain.

"You didn't have to use up that whole bottle on me, Mister Roberts," I told him after the shoppers expressed their sentiments then resumed their business. "But thank you just the same."

The empty bottle that had begun its journey in Lynchburg, Tennessee, tumbled out of Mister Roberts's hand into the galvanized dustbin beneath the counter. "Young man, if there's truth you can take to the bank now that this war is taking hold, it's that there will *always* be more liquor to be found somewhere."

My father nodded, his shining skin stretched tight by his grin. "He's right."

"Why is that, Mister Roberts?"

My father, who viewed himself as an open-ended student of the world and all who dwelled upon it, grinned more widely.

The shopkeeper gathered up all the glasses, for toasts in his shop weren't uncommon.

"I'll tell you why, Tally. Because how else can we manage to make it through such stupidity without becoming stupid, too?"

The previous war's survivors agreed, much as they hated to do so.

"We get by one way or the other," someone muttered as he picked out chewing gum. "We got to."

"Shell-shocked?" Mister Roberts asked him.

"Yup."

I learned something aboard ship: a man either becomes a true believer in utilizing armed force, consigns the whole business to the category of "necessary evil," or calls hokum and serves out his time in a disgust he barely allows himself the pleasure of feeling, except for when he's drunk or crying for his mama.

Some just leave, true. People designate them cowards, but I sure didn't have the guts to even consider it, even on the many days I wished I could have done so with no consequences.

In any case, that day, no true believers had come for Frum's three-for-two special. And we all knew the current drinking stupidity surrounding us originated inside the dark heart of a man named Adolph Hitler. We didn't know how bad it all was at that time, but when a country goes into lock-step, nothing good can come of it. We knew that much.

"Never mistake grandiosity for grandness," my father once told me. "Do your best and leave it at that, Son."

That day, however, he said, "I'll take some of that salt water taffy, Elmer."

WE AMBLED AWAY from Frum's through lacy Victorians, Craftsman bungalows, and right on into restrained Modernist ranchers and buttoned-up Cape Cods. Growing like cabbages in the garden of an engineer, rows and rows of siding-clad boxes lined up to receive whatever potluck the elements served that day. Most still radiated the builder-applied white paint, although optimistic yellow and Caribbean blue occasionally caught the eye.

We turned onto Valley View Road and the landscape took a breath as stone houses, built in stages of familial increase, sat comfortable in their pastoral surroundings.

"We just keep building things, don't we?" My father, whose woodworking skills in all styles were currently proffered by pricey local architects to their patrons, pulled two pieces of taffy out of his pocket. "Even in the middle of all that destruction overseas, look at all this. I sometimes wonder if we just can't help it."

He held out a piece to me.

"We tend to do better as human beings if we do." I took the candy, wrapped in wax paper, a product of Mrs. D. McPherson who stuffed them into Heritage Hill jars at any local businesses who let her in the door with one.

I placed one end of the twisted wax paper between my teeth, pinching the other end between my fingers, and pulled. The candy fell on the ground. "Dang it."

My father pulled out another one, handed it to me, then proceeded to retie his shoe as I tried again, cradling the palm of my hand beneath the confection as I twisted. There. I tucked the wrapper in the front pocket of my shirt.

Mmm. Wintergreen.

My father led us through the dwelling fields toward the state park, threading his hand into the crook of my left arm at the same moment I compressed the taffy against my soft palate with the belly of my tongue.

"As long as a person has a grateful heart and a good, honest mind, they can always find the best way. And you have a good mind, Son."

"Well, Dad, you taught me almost everything I know."

He pulled me closer to his side. "Except, clearly, how to give yourself a little credit for what you learned on your own in school." He shrugged. "Not to mention life."

"Maybe I have a little further to go with the honest part."

"Welcome to the human race, Son."

"I'd like to think at least my heart is grateful."

"Only you can know that for sure."

My father once told me a grateful heart, distilled to its essential nature, is simply thankful to be, and to be as made, placed in the situation it discovers itself again and again. He taught me thankfulness was a state of being, not an act of supplication. I'm still trying to understand fully what he meant because some days are easier than others in that regard. Some days being human feels like a little too much.

He stopped right in the middle of the lane we crossed, the wooden arch of the state park ready to welcome us. He held my remaining hand firmly in both of his. "What happened, Tally? Tell me everything you wish to tell."

He let go and we continued crossing the street.

The taffy flattened my following words and gummed up the pauses.

And because my father, who had never not loved me, did the asking, I told him all that I remembered in my most honest mind, including the fact my hand was blown off due to human error. "In other words, I got in the way at just the right second, Dad."

"What does that have to do with anything?" he asked with an unplanned smack of his candy.

"It was my own fault."

"What does that have to do with anything?" he asked again.

"It was my own fault, Dad." I swallowed a wad of disintegrating, sugary goo finally ready to go down.

"And again, Son, I ask you. What does that have to do with anything? Blame only serves to suck you back into that day to relive it over and over." Dad swallowed the entire wad in deference to the moment's importance. "Whether it's blaming yourself or others ... does it matter?"

"No. It really doesn't."

"Now, the good thing, Son, is that when you alone are responsible, you alone may offer yourself forgiveness, and you alone may receive it. Then, when you go about doing whatever it is you need to do following whatever it is that happened, you'll be a whole lot lighter. You don't need that kind of baggage. In this matter, you have only to be responsible to yourself. Isn't that right?"

"Oh, I am!"

"Then, there you go."

"What about people thinking I'm stupid?"

"Are you?"

"No."

He handed me another piece of salt water taffy. Light orange and a swirl of bright pink.

"This is pretty," I said. "I didn't know she made the swirly kind."

"Mrs. D. McPherson is branching out these days, I guess."

9

IN WOODS WALKED many times before by my father and me, he led me down a new path echoing the curves of a large creek to where an oak tree had fallen along the lip of the bank. He motioned me to join him as he sat down on bark the elements had been slowly flaying for what appeared to be years. While I lowered myself, he circled his fingers inside his jacket pocket. "As soon as I got your letter, I bought this pear for us to eat upon your return."

He held it in his palm. Fingers superficially divided by the scars of his trade curled lightly around the golden skin.

"That was two months ago."

"I know!" He laughed and crossed the fingers of his other hand. "I put it in the back of the cupboard away from the light and checked on it every day."

"What would you have done if it had ripened too quickly?"

"Well, Son, I would have eaten it with you in mind and

congratulated myself for such loving thoughts and good intentions. But it didn't, at least I don't think so. Now"—he extracted a bone-handled knife out of the front pocket of his trousers and slid it from its leather sheath—"let's find out how good this thing is, really." And he set the pear on my lap.

"But, Dad—" I picked it up.

"I'm about to piss myself, Son."

My father nimbly balanced his knife upon the brindled bark, then being a private person, strode behind me well into the woods.

I considered the pear resting in my right hand, its outward perfection, its lustered bulge and patinated brown stem. I considered my explicit imperfection, something important and irreplaceable that, no matter how hard I wished, how badly I wanted it, wouldn't be changed— no matter how hard I tried.

I could, however, assess the situation at hand. I could decide to accept responsibility for the pear's intended mission, or I could decide otherwise. Try or not try felt more like it, for whether or not I could accomplish this task on my own had yet to be proven. The mental exercise of dreaming up a plan couldn't hurt.

So, Tally, you can stabilize the pear *or* the knife, blade up, between your knees. On the one hand, *pun not intended, but there it sits regardless, and it isn't the most unfunny thing you've ever thought,* you will control the knife. On the other hand, you'll control the pear, but in this situation, you cannot control both to the same degree as before.

But is that true?

Is that really the case?

Wait. No. Not at all.

Stabilizing the knife afforded control and stability and I squeezed the handle firmly between my knees. Utilizing my truncated wrist on the dull side of the blade for added structure to the whole operation, I ran that ripened pear along the finely honed edge, cutting the fruit in two. Juice, freed from its jacket, gushed forth onto my trousers, its sweet aroma not lost in the forest air. I inhaled, closing my eyes, as both halves toppled onto my lap.

My father sat down and I handed him his half.

We bit down simultaneously, the translucent ivory flesh now giving up its nectar directly into my mouth, and, I assumed, my father's as well.

"A perfect pear, Dad!"

"Even though cut in two."

"I hear what you're saying."

"Too bad pears don't realize the sweetness they offer the rest of us."

"Do you think it would make it easier on them if they did?"

"Perhaps."

"But pears don't think, Dad."

"No, Son. They just make life sweeter for the rest of us."

The springtime woods receded as my mind flew to another place in time where first leaves descend yellow, supple. They fell clean and new though they had begun to die; they settled on the creek's delicate skin and raced away down toward the bay.

I shook myself to present, spring once more, remembering with her things come and things go, and new things sprout up in their place somehow.

Although my hand could never be replaced in the way leaves are—hand for hand—sprouting, tender, newborn flesh unfurling from the confines of my wrist, something new could conceivably arrive in that vacated space, something all for fresh possibility, for living in assurance that life always works out that way. Or I could choose to believe in an altogether irreplaceable loss. No blessings in disguise. No silver lining. No new season leading into yet another new season.

No thank you.

I bit into the pear again. Tasted its sweetness again. Came a little more to life again.

THE CREEK TUMBLED like silk as we ate the fruit. Two days prior to my homecoming, saturating rain had prepared what my nine-year-old lips once dubbed a "rushet" of water. Rushets, I decided back then, sped but did not overflow the banks hosting them. Rushets, enabled by an abundance of rain, gushed eagerly forward to empty out into the vast receptacle where they were bound to diffuse, to refresh, and to restore the toll the sky always takes for itself.

I could lose myself in them, mesmerized by the sheer power of water content to remain inside the open vein of Earth paved with smooth stones for quick travel to its dumping point. The flow became something of its own accord, powered by its very nature to seek the path of least resistance.

Meanwhile, the very molecules of water in front of me would congregate overhead and rain would fall upon Earth to bear her fruit for us to eat, because much of the time the Earth did exactly what we needed her to do, even if she didn't always play nice to suit our picnics and ball games.

My father assured me that Earth had own her ways, taking humanity less into her overall consideration than we think she should. "Forgive her, Tally," he told me after I learned about the Galveston hurricane, "and a lot of your questions about God will fall away."

As I sat with my father, the creek crested over submerged rocks and logs, perhaps car parts, oil barrels, maybe a chair or two, and who could know what else. The water swelled and stage whispered to anybody with ears to hear. I had never before emerged upon this stretch of stream from the wood forest. But my father knew about it or he could not have brought me here.

All of my life he took me only where he knew I would be safe or able to be guarded, guided, or taught outright. Yet he never stopped me from wandering on my own. And when my wanderings delivered pain or suffering as wandering off sometimes does, he bound up my wounds, cleaned up my face and hands, perhaps mended the knees of my dungarees, and invited in healing for as long as it needed to stay until wholeness resumed her place.

And back out I would go.

More often, the times I wandered on my own met me with surprise, delight, and joy. My father rejoiced if I wanted to share it with him. But he also knew the value of a secret, sacred spot, where a person somehow knows to love it alone is to honor its most intimate treasure.

"Every person needs a place like that, Son," he once

said, "to remind them the world was created for them, too."

A tree branch surfed down the rushet, easily gripped by two hands but not possible in one.

"I will never feel anything between my two hands again, Dad."

"That's a loss I can't understand. I'm sorry for that, Son." He threw his share of the pear core into the woods behind him.

"Why didn't I realize any of this before? Those are gifts."

"Yes, Son. But in a way, you are no longer able to take something simply because you can."

"That's true. I don't know, Dad. There's so much loss that when I think about how much, all the things I can no longer do, my head spins and I feel sick."

"Son, you have a nice strong will about you. Nothing forceful, but it's always gotten the job done."

"I see."

"How so?"

"A mountain is first moved in the mind. You told me that when I was ten."

"There is no other way a mountain can be moved by a human. With ease of movement, say, with two hands, we can manipulate on a whim—meaning without ample thought as to what we are actually accomplishing. We are capable of manipulating anything weaker than our own raw, physical power. You have now been relegated to the realm where you must either knowingly use *others* to force your will or apply more forethought as to how to solve your own dilemma your own way." He lengthened his legs in front of him. "And if you need others, Son, honoring their God-given rights in the process will serve everyone well, including yourself."

My father's carefully modulated voice always turned words too wise and to the point in circumstances still raw, into syllables full of goodness, kindness, and a belief rendering my ears capable of hearing the truth in them. That love, always flowing like rushets from his eyes, covered those words with the implicit, oft-spoken truth that I would never have to figure anything out without his help if I so chose.

"So, you're telling me the loss of my hand can hold its own form of meaning?"

"It's what you make of it like anything else. It may seem flippant for me to say it that way, I know. But in the meantime, as you calculate these things and life takes you to places where what you have decided is put to the test as either wise or foolish, whether or not you have a hand won't make a difference to that. A man becomes thick with transaction or transparent with truth. But he can never be both."

Because nobody enjoys being weighed and measured. And nobody values being used, no matter how much gold binds their wrists and ankles. My father told me that too. "And all it takes to go from using others to valuing them, despite the exchange of money, are two words, 'Thank you.'"

"Money is never enough?"

"It's fair exchange. The higher value is knowing that as humans we need each other, and if we do not appreciate those who have come to help us, we will never understand the value of ourselves. True service cannot truly be paid for, Son. All we buy is specificity."

"Well, I sure will have to find something specific. That might be all that's left for me."

"And I ask you, Tally, is that such a bad place to be?"

I thought about the world and all its possibilities, the fact that mine needed more focus didn't mean an infinite number failed to exist within them. "I just need to be able to see it, Dad."

"You will, Son. You will."

On the dark branches above, buds began giving way to leaf, and leaf would uncurl and stretch, mature and darken, thickening with time as all things tend to do. Where we now sat would be shaded for the summer heat. Dark green leaves would turn to gold, red, or wine, and settle into brown, dry effigies fit only for a tumble to the arboreal floor. The stark branches of winter, that which truly remained, would reach toward the heavens and feel the sun upon their skin because the light arrived in fullness once again.

If darkness overcomes the light, nobody will be around to know about it. But I remained after loss, watching leaves with my father. As long as I existed in this beauty, this grace, questions like darkness and light became mind play. I couldn't afford that anymore. Not that day and never again.

I laid aside my privileged theoretical philosophies for the practicalities of a life needing to be figured out.

"Dad. What never changes about a man?"

"The need to be whole, no matter what happens that

seeks to prove otherwise."

"How can we know what that is?"

"Remove the 'how can.' Remove the question mark, Son."

"We know what that is."

"Everyone does. *Why* we ignore it, maybe that's the question you need to ask yourself, Tally."

The creek sang as it went its own way. The sun dipped and we went our way, too.

I would just take it from there. And from there, I meant hope giving way to a greater reality, making a landing in some manner I never would have guessed otherwise. I'll choose trials turned to gold and beauty from ashes.

Crossing back into the Victorians I said, "I guess thinking of myself as a phoenix might be overstating it a little."

My father laughed. "Maybe. Maybe not."

11

M Y NAME, TALIESIN, *tally-essin,* became mine in 1922. Taliesin means "shining brow," a definition that conjures up a broad forehead. A magnificent inner light pours out through the same half-dollar-sized circle that draws my inner gaze when a question needs answering, a happenstance seeks resolution, or the wild hare of a pondering leaps about.

"Why that weird name?" I asked my father when I was twelve.

"Your mom and I thought of it as a light shining like a headlamp on a miner's helmet, piercing the darkness with a light so tenderhearted and pure all who feel its warmth are changed into the best version of who they are, and maybe who they came to be here on Earth."

I had no idea what he meant then, and even today it's still a bit obscure amid diapers, dinners, and dreaming up where to take the kids for summer vacation.

But I recognized some pretty high hopes in there. I never questioned its veracity because the people who ushered me here believed it about me first, believed me so capable of greatness they named me thus.

That my father believed this about every human being escaped me until aged thirty-five! What a belly laugh that gave me.

My father would have been perfectly named had *he* been named Taliesin, but his parents called him John—as many parents did back in the days when all babies wore gowns.

My father named me Taliesin—no middle name, because "with a strange name like that who needs one?"— after the Welsh bard who embraced a life that could rise to mythical proportions. We sat by the war memorial across from the city paper's busy printing shed when he told me, "Your mother first mentioned the name Taliesin because he was a man who used his words beautifully. You see, Son, swords are for those who no longer believe in the power of tongue or pen. Swords can only do one thing when used to persuade beyond threat. Words, on the other hand, can always be accepted or rejected as is every human's right."

The nearby pigeons didn't care about any of this. They left their droppings on shed and statue alike. "I understand, Dad. But what about using swords when someone is coming at you with a sword?"

"That, Son, is a question every human being must answer for themselves. And despite what you will hear one way or another, it's a question every human being gets to answer, no matter who likes the answer or not." My father believed free will to be a universal law. "I can't speak for the rest of them," he said one time with a sparkle in his eyes.

12

THE DAY I turned eight, my father started teaching me to whittle with a knife he had given me for my birthday. "This is a Buck knife, Son. No cheap practice knives. A blade is a blade, and a good blade is safer in the long run. Well, and the short run, to be honest. So, you might as well understand what that really means right from the start."

"Yes, sir." I nodded with a sober set to my mouth.

I felt proud to finally carry a knife around in my pocket. I liked the way it weighed down the fabric pouch inside my trousers. I liked unfolding it. And I liked the fact that if something needed cutting, I could pull out mine like my father did his and attend to the job right then and there. I could be that boy saving the day in an easy way because the world is actually built on small kindnesses. I could start following in my father's footsteps right away. From this day on, I could be a little more like that man.

Fifteen minutes in, the blade slipped on the cedar

branch my father helped me choose in the woods. Twenty minutes after that, he sat next to me at Dr. Woods's office.

The family doctor who had cared for me ever since I could remember entered the exam room.

"Donald," said my father, who had known him since their days in the service.

Dr. Woods swiped his dirty blond hair slant-wise across his forehead. "John. Good to see you. What has that boy of yours done this time?"

I held up my finger, loosely bandaged with a handkerchief. "Whittling. I got a knife for my birthday."

"You don't say. Well, the good thing is, it'll only get better from here, Tally."

"Yes, sir."

"Believe that," said my father.

Dr. Woods stitched my right index finger up tight without any anesthesia other than knock-knock jokes, because superficial wounds didn't warrant that kind of expense back then. That's how we learned to grin and bear it.

"Although, Son," my father said later that day as he laid my birthday dinner of chicken croquets, stewed tomatoes, green beans, and a small bowl of cucumber salad on the place mat in front of me, "the grin is completely up to you. That saying never made too much sense to me when applying it to real life situations."

The next day, the stitches served me well. Summertime showed wearing stars and stripes and my pals from the neighborhood gathered around me, asking if they could peek down into the dressing.

I said no.

"How did it happen?" asked several.

I shrugged, no big deal. "Cut myself with this."

I pulled my knife out of my pocket and into my curling palm in a flash before dropping it back in. Best to keep the curiosity going a little longer. A knife *and* stitches. Tally is a lucky guy.

The day's star shone directly down on me.

But that night on the porch when my father pulled out our sticks and began, my knife remained motionless.

"Not feeling like whittling tonight, Son?"

"Nah. I dunno, Dad. Those stitches really hurt."

"Do you want to learn how to do it? Really learn how to use a knife? Because whittling is about more than what you might be making it to be. It's about controlling a blade in all sorts of situations, becoming comfortable with it as a very handy tool."

"I dunno." Even though I did. At least I thought I did.

My father set down his stick/knife duo and took mine into his hand, cradling them loosely in a lopsided X. "Son, what happened yesterday was painful. But if you really want to learn how to use a knife, all that really occurred is the age-old truth coming to tell you this—everything takes practice, and those who find no shame in not knowing up front and experiencing the mistakes that tell them what *not* to do in the future, are those who learn best, most comprehensively, and by far the fastest."

What could a boy say to any of that?

"Your hand is going to heal, the stitches will come out, you'll have a scar and a tale to tell, and"—he leaned forward with a lopsided grin and a twinkle in his eyes—"trust me. You won't mind any of that one bit."

"The other boys thought my stitches were neat!"

He laughed and I did too.

He sat back. "But if you set these aside and you do so with the desire to learn how to use them intact, the real wound will be inside you—the kind of wound that stays open, the wound that says, 'I wish I had seen that through. I wish I had kept with it. I wish I had learned that well.'"

I nodded, tears burning my eyes.

"It's courageous to follow up on what you want, even if it takes a little finesse to get there. And being willing to face the risk you know by experience is there, well, that's what courage is all about. Do you understand, Son?"

"I think so."

He held out my Buck and the stick. "So, here's what I want you to do, and you'll be fine."

I nodded and reached for my duo, placing my fingers around that X as he did. "What do you want me to do, Dad?"

He leaned forward once more and whispered the words, "Just be more careful."

"That's it?"

"Yep. And one more thing. Anticipate where you're going to send that knife every time before you do. Picture the stroke, yes, but feel the control you're going to have, what pressure you're going to apply, what angle, and then do that. But feel it, Son. You've got to feel it ahead of time. Do you understand the difference?"

"Yes. Not just picturing."

"Not just picturing. Exactly!"

"And not moving over and over without picturing at all?"

He laid a hand on my shoulder and squeezed. "I think you now know all you need, Son."

I nicked myself once more a few months later because of an unexpected hardness I couldn't have foreseen, nor counted on. "That's life," my father said. "Nobody's immune to surprises."

I learned to control that knife; I learned to not let it control me. I carved some pretty things.

But maybe nothing compared to that pear.

13

B Y THE TIME we climbed our apartment staircase the final time on the day of my return, at least twenty people I knew had expressed happiness at my return. Some congratulated my discharge from the Navy with my life, if not my body, intact.

"It could have been worse," a few said, ignorant in a way that made me happy for them.

"I'm glad to be home," I said anyway, every time. And every time I meant it.

I have never once wanted to die. That certainty remained with or without my hand. Because sometimes an unforeseen hardness manifests in life, but you adjust your knife and keep on creating anyway.

And the quicker you pick the knife back up the better.

14

HIGH SCHOOL PUSHED me beyond its doors with playful punches on the arm. Promises of friendships for life genially died the moment we walked away. We accomplished what we were meant to, choice not factored in much. Here's the curriculum students. This is what you get.

I started choosing for myself that day as I made my way directly down the street to Selective Service. The bell slammed against the glass door from my quick-hard push, announcing my intent. The Navy called. Rolling horizon, glittering lights, and a well-defined purpose. Here's your life, gentlemen. This is what you get.

Not that I realized that then.

The opportunity was presented straightforward, workaday, and as my duty. In other words, nobody is falling over himself in gratitude at the sight of you, so get that out of your head, young man. I had signed on to be responsible, not regaled, to serve, not to be celebrated the general atmosphere of the storefront said in glass, linoleum and chrome. In my recruiter's defense, it had been a long day.

It didn't take long, and I walked back home by myself because if you need your father to enlist, you shouldn't. Or so I believed at the time. Maybe there was a little compassion in there as well. War, costly by any imagination's stretch, cost my father more than most.

When I joined my father back at our apartment afterwards, his chest remained the same size and his mouth uttered no patriotic words to stir the wintered dread that had settled inside me as something more *Gunga Din*. An actual war raged in Europe, and a lot of boys were busy dying in it. Boys we knew exactly like me.

Though a medic, my father got behind a Mauser one strange day in France and still bore the scars. While a father had to accept his son's enlistment, he had the right to do so without dramatizing a joy he not only didn't feel, but couldn't. My father knew better—that his only son wasn't just heading off to boot camp—I had signed up for war. The day, having begun its flight in sunlit celebrations on the high school steps, landed with a sober handshake from my father.

He remained strong, though, holding down all the lies I needed him to tell me that evening. I misunderstood my father's commitment to truth at times, but not that day. His own compassion fully displayed itself as well.

"Tell me what I need to do to make the next four years the most pleasant experience I can for you, Son."

"What do you mean, Dad?"

We sat in deck chairs on the side porch enjoying

momentous-sized bowls of Neapolitan ice cream. I always saved the chocolate stripe for last, he the strawberry.

"Well, Son, for the next four years you've chosen to have all your needs supplied in exchange for almost everything you are. The military only releases you from service if they have good reason such as death, incapacitation, or dishonorable behavior. So, considering the inability to exit at any time with impunity, you might as well be as comfortable as possible. There are things to enjoy, as well. Get in a company of good men and you'll learn things about being a human you won't learn elsewhere. You might get really good at cards. It's a terrible price you pay, though, in the end."

"But Hitler's gang, Dad. To be able to live with myself, I had to."

"As you say, Son." He scraped the pink remains on the side of his bowl with the edge of his tarnished, silver spoon. My father always got every bit he could short of licking the bowl. "I'm just saying you'll be tempted to focus on what's hard and painful, because we glory in that sort of thing. But people are people, and you'll still need a few around you to keep you sane."

"Do you not want me to be in the Navy?"

He pushed the bowl aside then gripped my shoulders. His eyes pierced mine with love as he leaned forward and looked into my heart as only he knew how to do. "Son, I honor your decision because it is yours, not my own made in the next generation. If this is what you are saying yes to, I will be the best father I can be considering your choices. It's what I've been doing since you grew old enough to make deep personal choices. And no matter what they are, I will always love you."

"I love you, too, Dad. I'm not doing this to run away."

"I know that, Tally. Thank you, though. But you never have to explain yourself to me in order to maintain my affection. Do what you think is right."

War is so pricey. Such a lavish and extravagant way to become a man. So *dramatic* and expensive when a week alone in the wilderness would do a young male human just as well, if not better.

"Mind a word of advice?" he asked.

"Go right ahead."

"When you don't like the way your commanders operate, or what's going on around you, keep most of your thoughts about all that to yourself and enjoy every single one for its own sake. Nobody tames a beast they don't know exists."

My father sent the best packages on base. His letters lifted me up on nights when I wondered what I was thinking the day I graduated, a world of choice suddenly laid before me, a world surrendered an hour later in the dried ink of my very own signature.

15

THE YEAR I turned fourteen, we drove to the cemetery to place flowers on my mother's grave. That day—breezeless, cold, and clear—the sun shone hard in the belittled atmosphere.

Low traffic allowed us to maintain the slow and easy pace of Saturday morning breakfast when my father poached eggs, fried up crispy bacon, potatoes, and lightly floured tomatoes, and toasted thick slices of fresh rye bread. Butter abounded. Sliced bananas in cream sprinkled with a little brown sugar and placed under the broiler for a minute and a half ended the meal because we usually had errands to run, and nobody stopped in anywhere to get hamburgers back then. "And besides. Looking forward to this giant Saturday breakfast gets me through all those workday bowls of oatmeal, Son."

The neighborhoods faded in and out according to the waves of immigration to our city, second only to New

York City. Bakeries and butchers, vacuum and shoe repair, tailors and florists, and a bridal boutique for good measure lined the streets. Restaurants with the colors of Italy on the signs bled into the blue and white of Greece, and neon shamrocks glowed from pub windows.

"I can't wait to drive someday, Dad."

"You never know what's going to happen when you have access to the wheel of a car, Son!"

My father's voice bubbled with youth, telling me of a curious little chore allotted to him as soon as he could drive a car. He lived with his parents in a detached, red-brick home downtown. Their property was bordered to the east by City Park, not far from the baseball field. My father grew up as the son of a successful builder and his socially compassionate wife: George and Keziah.

In the scriptures, Keziah appears on the list of patient Job's three beautiful daughters. My grandmother would not have been an exception had she been the original. She reddened her lips, had her shoes shined, and wore hairdos and seamstress-made dresses every day. Keziah pendulated her purse from the crook of her arm and levered her gloved hand at the wrist just-so. Having tuned her ear to her neighborhood long before my birth, my grandmother showed up whenever a person needed somebody. Keziah appeared each time appropriate to the need at hand, never her own. She arrived with mop and bucket, extra diapers and blankets, or casserole and yeast rolls. If the plumber and a checkbook applied, so be it. My grandmother used her voice, soft and musical, yet always intrepid, to take up for me always, even when my behavior failed to justify itself. "He's just a little boy, John." Or, "I don't think he's old enough to understand that yet."

She died my first year in the Navy. I never knew true heartache until then, the ache of mortal love untied too soon. My grandfather—confident, kindhearted, trusting in the way of goodness—passed six months later.

They loved me dearly and simply. Richly not lavishly.

George mostly built solid homes nearby. Beautiful homes. He hired craftsmen for pillars and balustrades, built-in bookcases and dressers, desks and cabinets. Believing in the power of steady improvement, his company installed exquisite trims, newel posts, and mantles in already existing structures. By the end of his life, George retired employees who never worked anyplace else. The man, given to a three-button roll, loved nothing better than pressing gold watches into a pair of working hands. Even a good pork roast and Keziah's mediocre watercolors couldn't come close.

Part of these craftsmen's job involved teaching my father after school. After a general education in all the areas represented in the company, he might have chosen bricklaying, stone masonry, concrete pouring, plasterwork, or laying tile to learn in-depth. But my father lived as beauty's troubadour, realizing humanity makes a way for her and does so consciously. He would do so with chisel and hammer. According to Keziah, nobody expressed surprise when he picked up woodworking and hand carving, eventually dreaming and designing all that mankind might possibly make from a tree.

"We had to reign in some of his grander ideas," my

grandfather told me before he died. "I told him he should become an architect, so that's when he began carving and sculpting in his free time." He shrugged.

My father chose the human form as his means of artistic expression. His obsession as a youth filled our home with wooden figures in poses from downright lifeless to sprung and ready, from stable and grounded to airy and whimsical.

"They're like children," my father would say. "Not like you, of course, Tally, but you know what I mean, don't you?"

I did. And it only assured me that if my father cared for his art so well, I would never be left out.

George planted the back yard full of rose bushes, no lawn remaining save for the walking paths between garden beds which Keziah trod each morning the weather permitted. She clipped roses from bushes he lovingly maintained and laid them in a large, flat-bottomed basket solely designated for the task. She arranged them bedside in hospitals and nursing homes.

Passions meet sometimes. My grandparents taught me that.

My father pulled onto the pebbled lane down which my mother's body rested. The right side of his mouth lifted. "When animals, mostly birds, injured themselves on one of the rosebush's thorns, Dad gave me the job of sheltering the creatures inside and nursing their wounds. That started when I was five.

"But then I turned fourteen. So, after my father had tooled around with me in the driver's seat long enough and he felt comfortable handing me the keys, your grandmother's deep need to delegate rewarded me the job of driving healed animals out to the country to let them go."

"You had to be responsible for injured animals? That sounds terrible."

"You think so? Well, I'm not squeamish." He laughed. "I just did as I was told."

"It's rather brave. A lot of people can't bear to see wounded animals. Or people, for that matter."

"Son, I have to agree with you. It takes less courage to destroy than it does to look upon the wounded and start putting them to rights."

"Did it ever stop becoming a chore? Helping those animals?"

My father took my hand. "It had to. For me anyway."
"Why?"

"Because that's the kind of person I grew up to be."

"But you fought in the Great War."

"There's something called duty, Son."

"A duty to kill other people? Did you kill other people?"

The one time my father took up arms almost killed him and I reminded him glibly at first convenience. To this day I would take back those words if I could. It wasn't my right. But like all words we speak, they hang in the fabric of eternity.

"You're doing a lot of thinking, I see." He opened his car door as I opened mine. Over the roof between us he said. "Duty, yes. Some might see it as that. But there are others of us, Son, and I don't know if you're yet old enough to understand the nuances here, who go in with the duty we feel for all of humankind, not just our country. We go in hoping to shed some light into the whole tragic system, because nobody really wants to go out that way, do they? Don't we all want to die in our beds, loved, at home? So anyway, some of us, well, we become cooks and medics and the like, and we clean up after people because someone has to do the good and basic human things, like keeping others alive, even in war. Can you see the meaning behind that? How that is good?"

I confessed to not ever having considered that.

"Think on it further, Son. Apply a higher meaning to every situation you can, and you will find some real unexpected treasures in fields you thought you already bought and paid for with your opinions alone."

By this time, we stood at the headstone of my mother's grave. In front of it lay a bouquet of mahogany roses he sanded and revarnished every year on her birthday.

I pointed to the name of Amanda Grace. "And the higher meaning of this, Dad?"

He slid his hat from atop his head down over his face for several seconds, pressed it against his heart, and turned to me with a control so quickly restored his expression needed a moment to catch up. "Your mother handed me the duty of a lifetime, Son: keeping another alive, doing the good and basic human things not for a company of men, but for my very own child, the person I would love the most for the rest of my life."

"But don't you miss her?"

"Every second of every minute of every hour of every day."

16

MY FATHER WALKED me to the train station the day I left for RTC. I planned on signing up to be a corpsman. "I remembered the rose story, Dad."

"That so?"

"Yeah. The animals and all."

"Oh yes?"

"So, I figured I would put people back together again."

"You won't get glory, Son. You know that, don't you?"

"Oh yes, I will."

And I hugged my father to me, son to father, man to man, corpsman to medic.

When my father pulled back, his eyes were full of stars.

17

ACROSS THE KITCHEN table I slid the test I had received back that morning in tenth-grade geometry. A turgid, practically glowing, red F sailed front and center over numerical figures made to bleed beneath the tears of Euclid. My assignment was to correct everything.

"I'd like to think we agreed to do this together," my father said.

"What? My math homework?"

"Yes. And all the other things, too."

A pot of soup simmered; foil-jacketed rolls warmed in the oven. I had already poured milk into our glasses and set the table.

Let the evening begin.

18

THE AROMA OF my father's dinner rolls still perfumed the kitchen though he had removed them from the oven thirty minutes prior. I'd actually dreamed about those rolls on board ship.

"So much of my hand was blown off, the doctors decided to just go ahead and remove all the metacarpals since they were so fragmented," I told my father as I fumbled my way through dinner, eating vegetable soup with my right hand.

"What did it feel like when it happened, Son?"

"I don't remember, Dad. Everybody said I remained conscious as one of my shipmates wrapped my arm in his deck jacket. I was supposedly responsive the whole way to sick bay. To be honest with you, Dad, I'm just as glad I don't remember. They did tell me I kept my cool, so I feel proud of myself, if that's allowed."

"If it isn't, I don't want to know about it," my father said.

"Me either."

He pointed to my now empty bowl and raised his eyebrows.

"No, thank you, Dad." I reached for another roll, contemplating if I wanted butter on it badly enough to ask for his help or figure it out on my own.

My father watched me intently, hand frozen next to his butter knife.

Now normally, one splits open a roll, scoops up a bit of butter with a dull, rounded knife, and spreads it. Possible, yes, but that required a necessary show to accompany it. No thank you. Think quickly, Tally.

Oh yes.

The objective, a buttered roll, needn't be accomplished in the manner of the pear, did it? I could adapt the circumstances surrounding its creation to suit my current ability to function.

With the roll kept whole, I dragged it across the current stick of butter we always kept softened atop the icebox now on the tabletop between us. My father slathered butter on anything he could. I raised my own eyebrows as I took a bite.

"Just the ticket, Son. How is it?"

"A lot more buttery, I can tell you that."

Dad plucked another roll from the basket, followed my lead and took a bite, chewed, and swallowed. "Definitely better."

Of course we ate our dinner rolls together that way from that day forward. Of course we did.

"I FINISHED YOUR new hand a few days ago, Son. It looks pretty good, I think."

"I'd be surprised if it didn't, Dad."

"What a nice thing to say."

20

Tʜᴀᴛ ᴇᴠᴇɴɪɴɢ, ᴡᴇ attached my new hand to the end of my wrist. He slipped what remained of my lower appendage into the leather cuff that held the hand in place.

"What kind of wood is this, Dad?"

"Live Oak. It's a hard enough wood for the job, but not too hard for me to delicately carve," he explained, buckling the straps around my upper arm and forearm.

"How did you render it so perfectly?"

"I watched you very carefully as you got bigger. I never wanted to miss even one thing as you grew."

The painted hand, curled in a loose fist, matched my flesh perfectly.

"I considered using shellac, but thought better of it. I'll just touch it up when you need it. I mixed enough of your skin tone for a half-pint jar."

"It's a beautiful hand, Dad. You should be proud of this work."

LISA SAMSON

"You're the thing I'm most proud of, Son. You could be getting through this with a lot less courage and nobody would blame you." He pulled on the last buckle strap—the final tightening—tugging twice gently, as if in farewell. What had been his to create had become mine to use. "Now, I do believe we got the length of the straps just right. Joe Gibb, the shoemaker, fabricated the cuff to my specifications."

"He did a really good job."

"Joe's the best." He smoothed his hand over the leather. "I guess it was finished before you even tried it on."

"We just didn't know it."

"Let that be a lesson to me," he said with a chuckle.

Yes, I thought, and to me too.

He pulled my sleeve down over the cuff. I turned my arm, moving the apparatus up and down, bending my elbow, raising it above my head from my shoulder. Something normal returned, quietly, like unexpected things do.

21

THE FINELY-CARVED HAND—KNUCKLED, fingernailed, embossed with tendons and bone—mirrored in form the perfectly-honed love given me all of my life, even more perfect than what I thought that day with my shipmates. Watching my father position the hand he had created, I realized this was absolute truth. I realized I needed to keep close to my heart this light, this love, this way, and shine it the same way he did, through love and goodness and service that said, "You should be here for all of this, you know. I know I am."

Few believe it's possible that a man like my father existed, even though we wish it could be so for every single human being that walks the Earth. I always thought people might deem me a liar if I told them about a being like him. I know what my father would say to that from his grave about any dawning of reality upon a person. "Until they don't, Son."

And so here I am.

I feel like everybody would be a little better off knowing about him, knowing they would have been loved by him, too. For in everything that can be, the opposite must be entirely possible as well, or we live our lives only as a moving picture for the entertainment of a mad, cruel, and voyeuristic deity. And to my knowledge, there is no such being meeting such a description. For madness is but for a season. But soundness? Love? Goodness? That is Eternal.

And it rings long after its bell has been struck.

22

THE PERFECTION OF my father's love in an imperfect world, by most human standards, audaciously arrived right where loss had set me down. My mother, having died before anything concrete about her might have solidified, imparted upon her leaving a deep knowing inside my physicality like atoms in mortar.

She loved me, too.

As she struggled to breathe through the pneumonia caught in the hospital after a miscarriage, my father promised to do the best job he could.

If Amanda stood in front of me now, I would tell her John kept that promise. And doubt wouldn't dull a single vibration of my vocal chords.

23

"**D**EAR DAD," I wrote two years into my service. "I think I would like to be a surgeon. Like you, I can keep my head around deep woundings and experience a supernatural desire to help in situations where most men lose their stomachs."

He wrote back. "You see the being beyond the flesh, Son. It's a must if you want to heal, not just repair the damage."

Healings mystified me. Each injury brought to me, or that I attended to right on deck, eventually became the wounded human being I followed up with that evening or the next day. And though I accepted every mystery residing inside them, for how can one not, the reasons they longed to be put back together belonged solely to them. I could only do the best I knew how at any given moment.

"It's all anybody can ever do, Son," my father told me in the eleventh grade. A guilt-inducing English teacher made me anxiously aware that disappointment in those around me sometimes centered on my performance or lack thereof. My father laid his pinochle hand face-down on the porch table. "If your best isn't good enough and *you* want to do better, Son, gain more knowledge or skill, perhaps, and see how that goes. If your best is never good enough for someone no matter how hard you try, you're probably not the man for the job, whatever that job happens to be."

"And that's okay?" I laid down mine.

"Son, what you have to give isn't always what someone else either wants or needs to receive. We're all made to be one-of-a-kind. There is nothing like another and I imagine it will always be that way."

"I'm not 'everyone's cup of tea?'"

"No." He smiled. "And you're not selling what everyone's buying either. Do you understand the difference between the two?"

"Yes. But why is that?"

"I guess the creation never needs to make the same exact thing twice. And some things go together and some don't and that's not a bad thing unless we decide it is."

And the conversation turned to human couples whereupon my father said, "Now right there, the one who you go together with? She's worth waiting for, Son."

"Was Mom that woman for you?"

"Indeed, she was."

"Did she feel the same way? Did she believe that love like that was worth waiting for?"

"I never asked her."

"Why not?"

"It was enough to know she got it regardless, and it was more than enough to know I was the man for that job. Your mother had a rough childhood, Son. I loved her wholly, and in that she was able to make herself whole again."

The man for the job.

I saw each sailor as the man for some job. I didn't know their purpose, and it wasn't my business. But I knew my job entailed keeping them alive, perhaps providing a place they could make themselves whole again and get on with it. I was a good cup of tea at those times, and if I wasn't selling what that unconscious man sought to buy, if I failed to buy him the ticket out he thought he wanted, I still had a job to do. Knowing from experience we sometimes don't know what's best for us, comforted me. Maybe living to see another day was exactly what he wanted, but just didn't know it yet.

24

FOR THE NEXT three months, I continued to heal physically and adjust to an existence that included loss of limb as more than a grim possibility. I learned to elude the world's eyes with my "trick hand" in play such that only the most observant among us might take notice, much like a magician navigates table, wand, and hat. The kitchen became my laboratory.

My father returned to the workshop a week after my homecoming. Each morning, he left a recipe on the Hoosier, the coordinating ingredients in the cupboards and the icebox, no expectation hanging like an order from headquarters. My father enjoyed cooking and eating and had no requirements about how they should go together.

After washing up the breakfast dishes, I would gather up the non-perishable ingredients, set them on the kitchen table, lean the recipe on one of the cans, and sit before it.

So then. How to manage this with one hand and a wooden carving.

Okay, now think. Prepare it in your mind, Tally. Every step ahead of time. You have plenty of that now.

Sometimes I dropped my head in my hands. Would the rest of my life feel like this?

"The problem is never that there isn't a solution," my father told me many times as he taught me what he knew. "Sometimes, it's that we don't ask for help when we need it."

"What if help isn't around?"

"That's a good question, because you're right, some of the time you have to figure things out all on your own. A lot of the time, when you come right down to it. So then at times like that, give yourself permission to find your own solution. Have patience with yourself as you move your way through the solution, step by step." At that point in my life, patience only made her necessary appearance while waiting that excruciating half hour until supper sat before me and grace had finished her descent upon our food. "Usually, one step leads to another, Son. And if you have time to think about what to do ahead of implementation, so much the better."

I considered each recipe step-by-step before beginning to cook, usually around four o'clock. The focus did me good, I can tell you that.

"Thank you, Son," my father would say if I'd readied the meal upon his return. Or, as he slid a pot or pan from its nested place in the bottom cabinet to prepare our dinner, "How was your day?"

And as he cooked, we talked of many things.

"Dad, are you happy with your work?" I asked two weeks after my homecoming as he deboned a chicken, something I had not yet mustered the courage to try.

"I am."

"You don't talk about it much."

"Wood carving has a nice outcome, but the process would be a little boring to hear about."

"Pun intended?"

"No. But that was a nice catch."

"What about your workmates?"

"What about them?"

"Do you ever have any problems with any of them?" Of course, some shipmates always looked for a reason to be upset. Did woodcarvers have them, too?

He shook his head. "We're all concentrating too hard to get into anything like that. Would you hand me that salt?"

I grabbed the shaker and held it out. "Whatever I end up doing, I really hope I can avoid the kind of trouble a person brings home with them and maybe even takes back out with them the next day."

My father salted the chicken and arranged the pieces to brown in the Dutch oven heating up over the blue flames. "Grievance is a heavy load, Son. I try to cast it off as quickly as possible."

"How?"

"Stay present to what I'm doing."

"That's it?"

"I don't know. But it's all I*'ve* got to tell you."

My father laughed and I joined in.

25

A T THE END of June, my father sat down to a chicken
pie. I'd filled it with peas, corn, mushrooms, carrots,
and finely diced onions. He'd forgotten to leave a recipe.
"Did you make this up, Son?"

I set out two forks and pulled out his chair. "It took a
little while, but yes I did."

"This crust is enough to bring a grown man to tears it
looks so good."

Our forks dove through the crusted pastry and into the
creamy filling, releasing its brothy scent.

He breathed in through his nose. "Now that brings
heart back into a fellow, doesn't it? Thank you, Son."

He took a bite, closed his eyes, chewed, then swallowed. "Just as tasty as it is good-looking."

I barked out a laugh.

Silence accompanied several more bites.

"What's next for you, Son?"

Because, if I could debone a chicken and make it into a pie, homemade crust included, my dreams remained in front of me. Sometimes his transparent mind rendered his inner bridges easy to cross.

"I want to go to school, Dad."

"Do you know where?" He reached for the small bowl of sliced cucumber at 2 o'clock.

We lived two miles away from a large university. "I think I'll stay in town. I was away with the Navy, so I know what it's like to learn things away from home."

"Big things at that."

"That's true enough."

"Let's get you enrolled next week. In the meantime, I will say it again,"—he closed his lips around the fork, slid the bite onto his tongue and chewed slowly—"this is a delicious chicken pie, Son."

My father was certainly right about that.

26

MY FATHER HELD little value for ownership for its own sake. He never did without, and I don't think he ever once viewed me as a cause for sacrifice. Meaning unlocked joy in expenditure for him as I found out that morning at the university when he enrolled me for my freshman year. We had lived small for a reason. At the registrar's counter he slipped a bank note from the chest pocket of his shirt bearing the full amount of my first year's tuition and handed it over, stars once more in his eyes, despite the heat wave miring the city.

As long as I could remember, my father and I inhabited a small apartment on the second floor of a white foursquare with additional side porches both up and down. Green shutters stood next to the front windows and the path-makers much preferred brick. We rented the left side consisting of a sun-catching kitchen, a blue-tiled bathroom, a tiny, cedar-paneled bedroom, and a living room with a fireplace that might have been put out if it realized it lived on an upper floor and not in a grand parlor. My father slept on the sofa beneath the large front window for as long as I could remember.

We lived in a place filled with light, routine, and the best of intentions if not always the perfect follow-through. We tried.

We sat at the kitchen table, a square piece of furniture he built just before marrying my mother. Cherry blossom carvings and a pair of robins adorned each hickory leg. If I counted up the minutes I'd spent tracing his work with my fingernail and charged the world for my time, I could buy a nice car. But the world doesn't pay people for that sort of thing. Nor should it.

Between the opening of the closed kitchen sheers, the July sun laid a stripe of itself on the black linoleum. Though an oscillating fan breathed across our faces, its breeze couldn't have possibly kept up with the perspiration that collected inside our hairlines and dripped down the sides of our faces.

"Someday, I want to buy you a house Dad."

"Why do you want to buy me a house, Son?"

"No reason, Dad. I don't know why I even said that." I wiped my forehead with my forearm as my father took out his handkerchief and dabbed at the same spot on his own face.

We frequently checked a thermometer topping one hundred degrees hoping for even a ninety-nine.

With slim expectations of truly cooling off that evening, we migrated to the side porch to catch the breeze because if a meteorological miracle would happen, surely it would happen there.

My father looked out over our street. "This place feels extra hot in the summer. There are a few days each summer I want to get out of here too. And this is one of them."

"I didn't mean anything by it, Dad."

"Oh, I know that." My father sat down on one of the old deck chairs my mother purchased at a secondhand shop years before. "Son, I appreciate the generous thought, but I'm home right here."

"But wouldn't you like a garden to till, maybe know that it's your land and not Mr. and Mrs. Williams'?"

Sitting to my left, my father grabbed my new hand and squeezed, its attachment to me enough for him, I guess. "Son, none of this belongs to us no matter how much you pay the bank. Do you see the sky? The water in the river?"

"I do."

"These things tell us in seeming contradiction that it all belongs to us."

"So, which is it?"

My father shrugged. "Depends on where you find your feet in any given moment. I know, let's take a walk to the park and get an Italian ice."

Who wouldn't agree to that? Lemon for me, cherry for him, we ordered from a carnival-themed cart set to close up soon and walk back to its own neighborhood. Perhaps the operator would end up surrounded by many familiar chairs and food that fed the soul and the body. And lots of colorful conversation. At least, I liked to picture it that way.

We walked along and ate our quickly melting ices.

He led us to the outskirts of our neighborhood to a small park consisting of a cement slab, a drinking fountain, and a sandbox no loving parent would set their precious child inside of.

"Which is it, Dad? Is it all ours, or is none of it?" I asked again as we sat on a bench and watched some boys play sluggish stickball in front of the city dump across the street. The gates, locked for the night, held back everything but the cloying scent of the discarded.

"We all die, Son. And all we thought we were, all we did, and all we collected to us belongs to anybody who claims it in one way or another. It all ends up in the dump. Either the *actual* dump or forgotten eventually by humans." He shrugged. "Unless you're Jesus or Genghis Khan."

"So, what does that mean for a regular person?"

"Oh, just hold things loosely,"—he pointed at the mounds of refuse, tires, furniture, building supplies— "except for the people who love you." One of the boys made a hit and his team cheered. "Love is the only real part of you you'll ever truly leave behind, anyway."

A female voice called out, "Boys! Time to eat!" And two lads, twins judging by their matching clothing, yelled, "Be right there, Mama!" The group dispersed with promises to meet after dinner, right there on the street that belonged to them—the street with the dump, the street sharing the same deep-fried heat with all the mansions all over town.

"I don't want to leave people behind in the pain I caused them," I said.

"Then don't," said my father.

"Is it really that simple?"

"Only if you want it to be. If you complicate love by raising your own desires over the well-being of others, of saying this deserves more love than that, my future deserves more care than those around me looking at me with real eyes, you will leave things behind that need mending."

"It sounds like an impossible dream. How can we keep from leaving sadness behind?"

"We can't help what our deaths do, Son. But we can make sure the life we lived will be missed in a way that lights a path, not one that requires healing. Do you understand the difference?"

"I think so."

"Here's a good rule of thumb, then. 'If you have a choice to value people or things, always pick people first.'"

"Do you do that?"

"I try my best."

It's all any of us can do, I guess.

27

"**D**AD, I WANT the last words I hear to also be the last words I say."

"I love you?" He nodded soberly. "Me too."

THE DAY OUR lateness for church required a sit-down in the back pew, I realized most girls required some type of hairdo or another. A *style* they called it. At fifteen, I finally took notice of curls, waves, straight curtains of hair, ponytails and rolls, bows, clasps, pins, and decorative combs. I didn't know what all was involved with hair styles, to be honest, figuring there had to be more than met the eye. The thought of that much responsibility to the outside world for what just grew naturally out of my head overwhelmed me. Is that what it meant to be a girl? How did my mother stand it? Who told them this was necessary to begin with? And why?

Running my fingers against my scalp, I literally thanked God the barber took care of all that one Saturday a month. Did girls ever just wash their hair and let it dry? I searched again. Yes. There sat Mary Williams, her hair a halo of black, the front held back from her vision with the smallest diamond pin.

After communion and a few good-byes to those who rushed out with us, we set to walking home at a good pace. My father had slid a roast in the oven prior to our departure, and the preacher decided to expostulate in a way that reddened his face, soaked through his shirt, and forgot about things like time and clocks. I don't remember what exactly had gummed up the reverend's path to the peace that passeth all understanding, and I'm not exactly sad about that. Several people squirmed when he talked about playing cards from time to time. Or going to dance halls. And that day, I can't remember which personal affront he confronted, but I think it had something to do with chewing tobacco and white lies.

"I'll bet sometimes you're relieved I wasn't a girl," I said as we hurried past Frum's, closed for Sunday.

"How so?"

"Hair, for one."

My father laughed and laughed. "Hair is just the beginning of those sets of differences."

"What are some of the others?"

He shook his head. "Oh, no. That's for every man to find out on his own, Son."

"Why?"

"Because there's a phrase you're going to hear a lot and I might as well tell you what it is. It's this. 'Women are all alike.'"

"I've already heard it. Maybe I was looking for a heads-up after all."

"Don't believe that lie for a second. Women are just as

unique as anyone. They're human beings in their own right, just as fit for life as we are. If you hear differently and run your life accordingly, prepare for a huge lesson about what happens when people use their God-given, free will in ways you least expected because you thought you already knew all about them."

My father saved me a lot of grief that day. I can tell you that.

And not just about women either.

29

T HE MORNING SUN transformed my father's felt hat from
black to gray, and the air sung that initial clear blue
note of autumn. He walked with me to my first day of
undergraduate classes at the university. "Things go a lot
smoother and feel a lot easier when you don't feel trapped
by your own decisions, Son."

"I feel that way about my hand, Dad. I was the one who
decided to enlist. I felt trapped at first, but I don't know, it's
given me a perspective on life that seems pretty valuable."

He took my arm in his. "You want to share it with me?"

"Blame is useless when there's nothing to be done. I
can't grow my hand back."

"No, you can't."

"So, I think I'm just going to give life my best shot
without it."

"Just say the word if there's anything I can do to help.
But you're a man now, and it's up to you to ask." He sighed.

"It's hard for me to even say that."

"Father knows best?"

"Compared to who?" he said with a chuckle. "Father knows better than to think he should run your life is more like it. Father knew his days of guidance were limited. Father knew the boy would eventually become a man."

"Thanks, Dad."

I filled him in again on the day's classes: American Literature, Chemistry, History of Civilization.

"Loved them all," he said.

"Why did you end up becoming a woodworker after the war?"

"Your mother said she respected men with work-roughened hands and I knew how to do it, so I made a change."

"She did?"

"She did. So, I figured I could keep working at the business and keep sandpaper in my desk drawer, or take to a trade I already enjoyed in my spare time anyway."

"What did Grandmom and Grandpop say?"

"They said, 'We're just wondering what took you so long.'"

We stopped at the walkway leading to the Science Hall. "How do you feel about that now, Dad?"

"Your mother seemed to have had a knack for bringing love into my life in all the best ways. I don't regret one minute I've spent creating beautiful things."

I loved hearing that.

He grasped my shoulders in his hands, squeezed a farewell, then said, "Supper's on me tonight, Son. Spaghetti and meatballs?"

"Best meal ever."

"I'll even get a bottle of red wine to celebrate." This said the man who only drank when life had already made him merry without it.

"Dad!" I called to his back.

He turned.

"What if it's more complicated? What if this is nothing like deboning a chicken?"

He closed the gap between us. "There's a heck of a lot more a person can do with a chicken than debone it, Son."

"That's true."

"You may find you like something far more than surgery. Be open. And remember, trying to prove something to yourself or others—*whatever the reason*—is one of the biggest traps a man can fall into."

"I don't want to live my life in any kind of trap, Dad," I said as people rushed round me at five minutes to the appointed hour of Beginning Chemistry. I felt their panic.

Dad grabbed my left hand. "Then don't." He leaned forward and whispered, "You have plenty of time to get to the classroom. And, Son?"

"Yes, Dad?"

"Never forget, not for one second, that *you* decided first that you belong in that room, not the professor, not the administration, not the other students. You."

"Why is that?"

"Because you mostly choose wherever you are. And you can unchoose, too."

"But what about giving up too soon?"

"Trust yourself to know the difference."

That felt like a tall order just then. "How?"

"We all know when we've hit a brick wall, Son. We just don't always recognize when the brick wall hits us."

I ASKED MY father why he didn't take the bedroom for himself and he replied, "I have the rest of the apartment when you're asleep, Son. You went to bed pretty early for years."

My third year of undergraduate work uncovered a keen interest in researching the chicken, not deboning it. We sat at the kitchen table on a winter night, snow falling heavily. The porch light illuminated the descending flakes, their dips timed with the faint music from the records my father played in the evenings. I studied as he read from a collection of various poets the world over.

"Would you like to trade places?" I asked. "Have your privacy again?"

"Son, I stayed out here when you were in the Navy, didn't I?"

"That's true. Why?"

"I like it out here. I always have. Out here I sleep in

the echo of a lot of good times."

I couldn't argue with that.

"And you know what else?" He rose from his chair to make our nightly pot of tea. "I fall asleep when my head hits the pillow and sleep hard and good until I wake up seven hours later. Does it matter, in practical terms, where that happens?"

"Not that I can see."

The familiar sound of water hitting the bottom of the kettle, the hiss then the pop of the ring of the gas burner igniting, joined with the hushing of the accumulations of snow. Add to that the soft whine of the radiator, and contentment seeped into me. This nocturne of habit, every bit as beautiful as the Chopin playing from the living room, I accepted lovingly, even as I had always been accepted, just as I was, in any given moment by the man over there spooning Luzianne into my mother's porcelain tea pot. My father, content in himself and content in who he was given as a son, lifted cups from the cupboard shelf for each of us with a quiet joy.

And I knew it.

I knew it.

"Where did you get that couch, Dad?"

"Your mother picked it out when we first got married."

"Ah."

"Yes, Son. Exactly right."

31

IF WE CAN'T be with someone, can it be enough to be with what they have loved and leave it at that?

Every day my father said yes to that.

And I am living proof.

O N UNDERGRADUATE GRADUATION day, my father and I
set out for the train station. The first four photos on
the new roll of film placed into his camera that morning
captured me walking across the stage, shaking hands with
the dean, tossing high my mortarboard cap, and finally,
mugging for the camera, arms slung across the shoulders of
the two closest friends I made: Jeanine Franco and Robert
Mills. They mugged too.

No signing up for the service this graduation day. Not
that they'd have taken me up on an offer.

We ventured forth into the unknown.

My father packed a drawstring bag full of snacks
and supplies: apples, two packages of mini cereal boxes,
powdered milk, two spoons, a bag of hard candy and two
telescoping water cups.

Each of us strapped a duffel to our backs stuffed with
two sets of clothing, some extra drawers, socks, and a towel.

The most basic of toiletries: deodorant, toothpaste, a tooth-brush, a comb, razor, and a bar of soap barely weighed us down. A small pillow and a rolled flannel blanket secured to the top of the duffel assured us of some sleep when no beds showed up for the taking. My father carried his Buck knife, a bottle of aspirin, a small container of hydrogen peroxide, and a tin of Band-Aids; I toted a lighter, my own Buck knife, needle and thread, and some twine.

The station, freshly scrubbed, echoed with the force of our heels against its hardwood floors and all benches remained vacant, save one. A young couple in Sunday best, too young, sat with clasped hands between them pretending to be grown-ups. Maybe bound for Vegas, or Elkton.

"Let's hope they really do find the answer in one another," my father said as we stopped in front of the ticket counter. "Here's wishing them the best."

The train arrived and we embarked with the signature spring that outsets deliver. We had our pick of the seats after the sweethearts decided to venture into their own car. We both fell asleep until the train stopped at the next station.

After disembarking, my father and I inspected the board for outbound trains. "Looks like the next train leaves in ninety minutes. Long enough to get a bite of dinner."

He purchased tickets to a smaller city several hundred miles away. "There's a lot of beautiful architecture there as luck would have it, Son."

So, we ate at a nearby train-car diner, polished and reflecting the gloaming. My father ordered the hot roast beef sandwich with mashed potatoes and green beans, while I settled on meat loaf, mashed potatoes, and peas. We finished up with heavy slices of fruit pie and tall glasses of fresh, cold milk.

"What if we want to get off the train sooner?" I asked.

He shuffled through a single-folded stack of bills and pulled out a dollar and tucked it under the sugar shaker. "If that's what we really want to do, Son, then that's what we'll do."

We found seats on another sparsely populated car.

"Train's going to take all night to get there. Lots of stops along the way," he told me.

"I think it's going to be a pretty sunset tonight."

My father loved watching the skies.

After the display of roses, fuchsias, deep lavenders, and royal gray split by blushed light faded, we called it a night, releasing our pillows and blankets from our sacks. The conductor turned down the lights and I gazed out the window into the darkened expanse.

"Do you see Polaris, Son?"

"I do."

"That's good."

And my father fell asleep just like he said, quickly and into such a depth I wondered if maybe he traveled to the North Star and wasn't allowed to remember the trip upon awakening to the light of our own dear and reliable star.

We have no name for it. It is truly a sun among many suns. But it is ours.

33

IF I TOLD you my father's face had been burned in The
Great War, and if I told you he wore a widely brimmed
hat to keep it in shadow when he could, would you think
any less of him?

34

W<small>E PULLED INTO</small> the next station at 7:30 a.m., gathered our belongings, and placed them neatly in our sacks. Ready to go.

When we stepped onto the platform, I asked my father, "Should we have some cereal before we head into town?"

"I'd rather find some bacon and eggs, Son. How about you?"

"I just thought we'd save some money."

My father patted the sack of food. "This is at the ready for when money doesn't matter, even if we had a million dollars in the bank."

"Okay. I think I see."

"Except for the candy."

Of course.

My father enjoyed bacon, eggs, and two pieces of rye toast with jam. I surrendered my hunger to pancakes swimming in maple syrup and sausage patties cooked crisp. The waitress took note of my hand. "You lose that overseas?"

"Yep. I sure did."

"Still feeling pain?"

"Some days. But the worst is over."

"Glad you boys are home now. Breakfast on me, men."

My father said, "Just his. I didn't do anything."

"Meaning no disrespect sir, but how did you come by that face?"

Oh my, how we laughed, my father and I. She joined in. It was a miracle if you ask me.

35

M Y FATHER AND I established one rule for our sojourn two days into the trip. "No shame in creating a little structure for yourself, Son." We called it *The Next Train*.

When we felt the urge to disembark, we did. We would check the boards. The next train could be minutes from leaving the station, or hours, or sometimes, the next day.

Wherever it headed, we joined in. We had a lot of laughs and ended up spending more than a few nights with drifters. My father remained the same no matter the company.

We toured small towns in greater detail, bunked in nearby motels or boarding houses—in one case eating dinner, breakfast, lunch, and dinner once more before the next train slowed its wheels and stopped long enough for my father and I to hop on. The conductors seemed very surprised to see us as we climbed up the steps. No need for the formalities of "All aboard!" at those stops.

We took in a few prayer meetings, a couple of ball games, and wandered through town museums. We read about local heroes, the illustrious times presidents spent the night, or the passing by of a funeral train of someone famous. Photos of the iron horse and its cars draped in black crepe were displayed behind glass. We learned about battles, dam breaks, agriculture, factories, industrial barons, and in one case, a famous circuit-riding preacher born and bred right down that very street. "In a whorehouse to boot," I said.

"Where did you hear that word?" my father asked.

"Oh, Dad. I'm twenty-six years old."

He laughed and refrained from asking if I knew about them firsthand or hearsay. You have to give a man credit who can mind his own business even with his son.

The cities passed us by, mostly due to the frequency of outbound trains.

"We live in a city anyway," said my father. "I don't mind seeing the small towns and countryside one bit."

"I don't either."

We sucked on hard candy to pass the time; we slept on station benches, in hay barns, and under the stars; we ate our cereal and apples. And all the while I felt safe. I didn't want to be anywhere else right then. Having worked hard to graduate with high honors, I wanted to honor my father's gift to me—not his investment, not his sacrifice—because to a man like my father, nothing he did for me began as either of those things. And neither did this trip.

All of this because he loved me, and love of all things

is to be most honored. In the honoring, I guess I loved him back, and something felt very holy, very clean about letting it be that. The sound of his breath as he slept, the slackness of his cheek above the blanket tucked up to his chin, the dart of his eyes as he dreamed of things I knew nothing about unless he chose to share them. And he loved me most of all.

36

M Y FATHER TAUGHT me that ideas were but starting points, and bad ones need be nothing more. Unfortunately, we are taught early to accept bad ideas that already exist in ways *we* can see and feel aren't up to any good, but many others cannot. So, we figure they must be right.

"Do you ever get mad at the people who think killing each other is such a good idea that you ended up in France?" I asked him as we sat by a field near a bright red train station. The white fence kept in goats and donkeys. We leaned against the gate.

"What would be the point of that, Son?" he asked.

Because he taught me to think before answering, I did so. For the next three hours I ushered my mind down many trails of thought, and at some point, the winsomeness of my heart, the deep part of it, jumped right onto the path.

We had boarded a train, lucky to have found two seats side-by-side. "I have an answer to your question, Dad."

He set down a book on Capability Brown. "I'd love to hear it."

"There's nothing rage can accomplish that love in the exact same circumstances cannot do more efficiently, sufficiently, and with greater permanence."

"There you go, Son. Better than I could have said it."

"So, do you blame anybody when you look at yourself in the mirror, Dad?"

"I used to. I landed last at blaming myself, and I suppose we all do that at one point. But I don't do that anymore."

"Why is that?"

"I came home to heal and your mother was my nurse."

"You might have met her in a host of other ways."

"But I didn't, Son."

"No. That's the truth, isn't it?"

"And to fight with the facts of the past? Nobody else's ideas are worse than that."

37

"**D**AD, WHAT DO you think of hope?"

We sat in a city station, floors slick from the rain tracked in by passengers now progressing with vigilant ankles toward their trains.

"I'm all for it. Why?"

"I don't know. I've just been thinking about it."

"So, what do you think?"

I reached into the sack and selected two pieces of hard candy, offering my father first choice. "I wonder if having hope, too much of it anyway, is akin to a person who is ungrateful for what they have."

"That's one way to define it." He popped a sour cherry candy into his mouth. "Not my personal definition, but I can follow that train of thought."

My father, once I became a man, only gave his opinion when I asked for it. He once said, "How will you find out for yourself who you are if I'm the one who thinks he knows it already?"

"So how do you define hope?" I asked.

"Believing tomorrow is going to be just as good as today."

"Isn't that faith?"

He cracked the candy between his molars. "Not to me. To me, faith is believing without a doubt the good will happen, even when death is on the day's agenda."

"Like days when you lose your wife?"

"Or your hand?" he asked.

"I've done just fine without it, Dad."

Oh.

Dad took my live hand. "It feels different to say it about a person than it does a hand, though, doesn't it?"

"Yes."

"What if we accepted death?"

"Did you, Dad?"

"The choice to live was easy for me, Son. I was still alive. You were still alive. There was no bearing on how much I loved your mother in my decision to accept her passing, but every bearing on how much she loved me. And you. Do you see?"

"Can it really be that simple?"

"Yes, it can. That doesn't mean it always is. And it doesn't mean it doesn't hurt. But people do get to choose that, Son."

As we sat waiting for our train, I realized if one human being was capable of that kind of acceptance—the proof being his love for me—the daily challenges of life could be accepted and dealt with much easier. At least on the inside.

"Are you afraid to die, Dad?"

"No. How about you?"

"I'm not afraid of death. I am a little scared of *how* it might happen. I really don't want anything violent and prolonged." As if anyone does.

Forty minutes remained until the next train's departure. Lucky enough to have found a spaghetti dinner at a nearby parish raising money for a new roof for the school building, we now sat with our pockets weighed down with bread one of the school sisters rolled in a clean cloth, as well as a can of sardines and a jar of olives. Readying for an all-night chug through the mountains, we both looked forward to the rocking slumber we had become so familiar with.

"Well, I can give you a few tips that *might* lessen the chances of that kind of earthly departure."

"Okay. I'd like that. Just a moment, if you don't mind."

I dug into my pack and pulled out my notepad. "Okay."

My father laughed. "I feel like the pope or something, but all right."

1. Mind your own personal business whenever and wherever you can.
2. Take care of yourself and your own as much as is possible for you.
3. Help those needing it who come across your path.
4. Don't confuse opinion with service.
5. Realize there's more to people than meets the eye.
6. Speak the truth as enlightenment, not attack.

7. Don't agree to anything you know you won't follow through with.
8. Do what you say you will do, or let the person know if you can't and why. It's called common courtesy.
9. Never lose control of your faculties, speech, or movements.
10. Forgive.
11. Don't assume you know when you can't possibly do more than assume.
12. Be grateful for what you have.
13. Know who already loves you and be content with them.
14. Meet strangers in public places.
15. Have faith.

I pulled out that sheet of paper many times over the years when I needed guidance and something on that list always applied. More than vague theory, he had found it to be true. But I sought to guide my own life well, and my father's wisdom served me likewise.

When I had my own child, I realized it could be summed up in the words of Socrates and Jesus:

Know who you are.
Treat others as you would like to be treated.
Love God. Love your neighbor as yourself.

When we disembarked at the next stop, the midday sun poured through the soaring Palladian windows of the limestone station. We searched the board for the next train, and before I could think about it, I said, "I want to go home."

Without hesitation my father said, "Let's go," took my arm, and ushered me out of the station doors leading to the street. We immediately walked to the cab stand.

"What are we doing, Dad?"

"We're going to the airport, Son."

"Okay. Why?"

"Because when it's time to go home, you head home."

38

WE CARRIED OUR bags up the stairs to our apartment, the familiar smell of the entry hall a welcome in itself. My father set down his burdens to fish his house key out of his pocket. As he swung open the door, the clock on the buffet in the living room greeted us with twelve tinny clinks.

We threw our things in the corner of a brand-new day and went straight to bed.

The plaid coverlet on my bed smelled fresh somehow, and the mid-summer air floated from the open window across my sun-soaked face as I slept, happy to be exactly where I felt most comfortable.

When I asked my father the next morning about our quick return he said, "A lot of people will tell you the journey and the homecoming are one and the same. I love journeys, Son. Big, small, it doesn't matter. But coming home? Well, there's nothing quite like that is there?"

"No. There isn't."

"So, when it's time to go home ... go home. And do it as quickly and as safely as possible. But get there. Don't stop until you're tucked in your bed."

"Or your couch?"

"Or your couch."

I enrolled in medical school three days later.

"There are many ways to be a doctor, Son. I'm proud of you."

B Y THE TIME medical school came to a natural close, my father had begun to slow down a little. He still walked to work where he carved mantelpieces and newel posts in detail as his primary employ. Every so often, he brought me to his workshop to see the flora, fauna, swirls, and waves that danced out of his hammer and chisels.

"Dad, these are beautiful!"

"Well, Son, if you exist long enough and decide to live by what you love, everything pares down to a thing of beauty."

"I'm pretty sure this requires skill as well."

"True. I guess I just opted for a simple life. The opportunities to be ill at ease are fewer and farther between, and I like it that way."

Having decided long before not to pursue surgery, I was certain the subsequent research in a laboratory setting devoid of the very people I wanted to help would fail me.

My father and I differed in this. While quietly creating beauty fed him, availing myself to others in need fed me. I didn't always care about lessening my opportunities to be ill at ease, but I knew peace could still be maintained regardless. Spending my life in a laboratory felt just like that brick wall. Twenty-nine years old when I graduated from medical school, my certainty of the future remained as elusive as ever. I was set to start my residency at University Hospital in two weeks.

We sat on the porch playing Parcheesi.

"Will my life ever come fully into focus?" I asked.

"You don't have to know yet, Son."

The beginning of September brought some relief from the heat, and the maple tree across the street started blushing at the tips. "You're taking the next step. It's all you can really do, Son. It's all any of us can ever actually do."

"And if we don't?"

"You mean if other people don't?"

"Ah."

He smiled and nodded, that particular lesson—that judging what we are choosing to experience in light of the incomplete and theoretical perception of other people's choices constitutes a recipe for personal confusion—was shorthanded by the knowing in our connecting gaze. That lesson seemed to come up a lot, truth be told.

"Looking right, left, and over your shoulder takes your eyes off the road, Son. Simple as that. Believe me, I have tripped over the rocks and rubble on other people's path, but tripping over my own feet feels a whole lot easier. And yet"—he threw the dice—"the ground I always fell on was my own."

"I can't imagine you tripping like that."

"That's because you didn't know me when I was seventeen."

40

"Who wants a one-handed doctor?" I despaired one evening as we drank our tea.

"Someone who doesn't ever get to be treated by a doctor at all?" my father suggested. "Someone who doesn't need a perfect doctor to experience proper treatment? Someone who would look on your loss as coming with some valuable lessons that might do them good, too?"

He went on like that for a good while.

41

MY FATHER'S WORDS returned many times over the next three years, particularly on days my prosthesis highlighted my inabilities when compared to the other doctors. On those days, a population of ragged, bony, and sore people welcomed me in my imagination. And they trusted me because, face facts, all of their other options had been stripped or never offered in the first place. In other words, I was better than nothing.

My residency almost finished, many of my colleagues received worthy offers, while all my first interviews became last interviews.

Perfect grades.

Solid credentials.

Traveling overseas for work in epidemiology and treatment in third world conditions had no effect other than a personal interest revealed on the part of the interviewing physician. My father's words certainly rang true in rudimentary places where no water ran through pipes and simple infections stole sight and limbs. Each day I gave out relief, stars fell back into people's eyes.

No takers over here, though. University Hospital offered me a job, to their credit.

The last hospital on my list having rejected me that afternoon, I set the supper table. "I want to try something new, Dad. Go to a new place. What do you think of that?"

Dad slipped a roasted chicken from the oven by the handles of the pan and set it atop the stove. "The bird is done, Son," he said, ignoring my question.

I carved the chicken to nine pieces including the back and put a breast on each of our plates.

"No, Son. We're going to eat the whole darn bird tonight."

"Really?"

"Yes. No holding back. No worrying about leftovers."

"Why?"

"Because the time for chicken metaphors has come to a close. You're ready to serve. There is a world of people out there who are no stranger to lost limbs and missing hands, or maybe they're just sick and they need you, particularly you, and I think you know why."

"Dad, right now I don't. I'm pretty discouraged."

"You asked me what I think about you going to a new place." He put two fingers on my heart like he had done many times as I grew. "This right here. It's called compassion. It's called empathy. It's called caring enough to do something. Do you understand how powerful that is, Son?"

I did. God help me I did. I had been living with the

prime example of that all my life.

"Will you come with me wherever I go?"

"Oh, Son. I'm always with you, even when you can't see me."

Real love never goes away, he told me many times when I felt the absence of my mother.

"Real love never goes away," I said.

"It just can't, Son."

42

M Y FATHER ACCOMPANIED me to the hollows of the mountains two weeks later. I drove while he commented on anything of note his side window displayed so I wouldn't miss it completely.

"That pond was just bobbing with mallards."

"Smell that freshly turned field?"

"Somebody at that house sure knows their way around a set of hedge clippers."

"How cows get to the top of a manure pile as big as that one I can only guess at."

"That little place would be fine with a little TLC."

"What kind of dog was *that*?"

We stopped at roadside stands. We snapped photos of historical sites. We journeyed to Green Mountain Free Clinic featured about a year before in *LIFE Magazine*, run by my undergrad school chum Robert's Uncle Jim. The photographs had haunted me ever since: minimal life seemingly impenetrable against good fortune, toddlers with a set to their mouths, and mothers who had lost the stars in their eyes a long time ago. I'd set up an interview on my own initiative in answer to the question my father posed one night as we drank tea and played Scrabble, that question being: "Where do you think you can do the most good?"

That clinic burst into my mind with a flash of yellow.

A lot of other fellows wounded in the war ended up on its doorstep. The mines rendered their own brutality. Many had lost limbs; some had left a portion of their minds overseas or in the deep darkness of the earth. Though great in number, they represented a small percentage of those requiring medical help.

"The point is, Dad, Green Mountain Free Clinic comes face to face with all manner of loss and most of the patients live in poverty."

We stayed in a small roadside motel called The Pines.

My father threw his suitcase on the bed. "This reminds me of the place your mother and I stayed at on the way home from our honeymoon."

"Good memories?"

"Son, this room reminds me of getting stitches. You just have to grin and bear it until you're on your way again. I think your mother would agree."

He slept just as hard as ever.

43

"You're the perfect man for the job," Dr. James Hill said after we chatted, his conversation broken in like a pair of favored work pants. "I'm ready to head to Florida or somewhere. When I got your letter, I said to my wife, 'Get a new swimsuit, sweetheart, we're about to retire!'"

I laughed.

When I climbed back into my car, Dr. Hill shook my hand. "We'll be seeing you soon, Doc. You won't get rich at this. You know that, right?"

"I do." And I shook his hand in return.

Gladness erupted then, as it had years before. I could still shake hands.

44

I TOLD MY father everything sitting at the window table in a storefront restaurant. Parker's specialized in *Hometown Cooking at its Finest*. If soup beans and cornbread tasted better elsewhere, I wasn't about to go looking.

The excitement of getting the position recounted, I finished up with that handshake.

"It's good to shake a person's hand," Dad agreed.

"Why?"

"What do you mean, Son? A handshake is a hand-shake."

"Is it good because it tells you something about a person?"

"No. It feels good to have a ritual, even among the most hardened of us, that brings us together physically."

"I feel like I can tell a lot about a man by his handshake."

"Like what?" My father slathered butter on top of a steaming-hot five-by-five-inch square of cornbread.

"Well, if he wants to dominate you for one."

"Oh, the firm handshake that almost brings tears to your eyes?"

I laughed. "Exactly. I always think, 'Hey, Mister, I only have one of these left so ease up, all right?'"

My father smiled. "Maybe he just doesn't want to lose control, give up anything he's afraid he might lose. Maybe it's not about domination, but preservation."

"That could be it too."

He cornered the tines of his fork into the cornbread and pulled away a bite. "It could be a lot of things, I guess."

"Now, that is true."

"How's that catfish, Son?"

I had yet to take a bite. The fish fell apart and finished its surrender in my mouth. "Delicious."

"May I?"

I nodded and he tried a bite too. He bobbed the fork over the fish. "Stick with knowing what you actually know, Son. Anything else is a guess, and you might as well go ahead and confess to it so you don't cheat yourself when the truth shows up eventually. That's delicious catfish by the way."

Cornmeal breading and deep-fried just right.

"Yes, it is."

We both knew it.

I looked back on that conversation as the most precious gift he ever gave me as a doctor, a father, a husband, a man, and a human being.

Know what you know, not what you think you do.

45

I WASHED UP the Saturday morning dishes two weeks
later just before we set out for a walk to Frum's and
some groceries. We'd gone all out with fried potatoes and
ambrosia. Dad finished up the crossword puzzle left over
from the previous Sunday's paper.

"I really would like you to move down with me, Dad."

Dr. Hill decided on a mid-August start just in time for
the changing of the season. "The town'll be getting ready
for school, finishing up visits to family for the summer, and
what not," he said, knowing all I didn't about life in Green
Mountain.

"Leave the city?" my father asked.

"Yep. You and me."

"Why is that, Son?"

"I just love you, Dad."

"That's all?" He began to gather the used cutlery.

"That's all? Is there a better reason than love?"

"Using your old man's words against him?"

"If it's appropriate."

He laid our forks and knives next to the soapy sink. "I'll have an answer for you by Friday."

"All right."

"And I love you too, Son."

46

E VERY SO OFTEN in the middle of the night when I used the toilet or poured a glass of milk, I witnessed my father weeping over the small photo portrait of himself holding Mom's arm on their wedding day.

His dark suit sported a rose boutonnière, and a pearl-topped pin pierced her pink lace dress to hang a gardenia corsage high up near her shoulder. Her gloved hands, a bit large for a woman that small, cradled a petite, white prayer book with gardenias, rose buds, and satin ribbons on top. Their eyes shone with stars.

Their smiles contradicted the traditional pose as laughter stretched their faces beyond formality. Instead of looking at the photographer, they had focused upon my father's little cousin, four-year-old Sam, who had curled his fingers around his lower teeth and pulled down on his jaw as far as he could. Cross-eyed. Good job, Sam, I always thought.

Even as a youngster, I recognized the holiness in their communion. And I recognized the holiness in his honest-hearted remembrance of it.

I really learned how to control my bladder because of those nights. And I can close doors without a sound.

47

"What kind of ice cream did Mom like?" Choc‑olate.

"What was her favorite color?" Two of them, yellow and pink.

"Was she a good cook?" Very. But not fancy.

"How did she do in school?" She never said.

"Did she enjoy card games?" Only two‑player ones.

"What made her cry?" Great beauty.

And on and on.

One day, when I was nine years old, I laid out four sheets of paper along the kitchen table, readying my activity for the evening. I plucked a pencil from the kitchen drawer.

"What are those for?" my father asked, looking up from his book, a manual on Bavarian motorcycles.

"I want to ask you questions about Mom and write down the answers."

He pushed the manual aside. "Why do you need to

write them down when I'm right here?"

"I just thought it would be better if you didn't have to repeat yourself all the time."

"Oh, I don't mind."

"Really? You don't?"

"Not at all. In fact, I like answering your questions."

"Over and over?"

"And over again."

I tapped the pink eraser on the table top. "What about when you die someday?"

He howled with laughter. "By that time"—he thumped my chest over my heart with his middle and ring fingers—"it'll all be written right there."

"Is that true?"

"Yes, it is. You see, Son, when a person has truth written upon their heart, it never goes away."

"And why is that?"

"The heart, that place where your love abides, only allows for the truth in the first place."

"Like Mom's hair color?"

"That's more like a fact."

"So what truth are you talking about, then?" I asked.

My father took both my hands in his. "That she loved you every bit as much as I do."

"That sounds very true."

"I know it to be a fact."

"How so, Dad?"

He squeezed my hands. "She wrote it on your heart herself, and Son, that's the thing that matters most."

48

FRIDAY CAME, THE day my father would declare a decision on whether or not to take up residence in Green Mountain. He returned from work at the regular time of 5:15, slid on his boots, and left in the blistering heat for a solitary walk in the woods. By this time, I had already assumed his decisioning pattern when circumstances clouded up my line of sight.

Ask all the questions you can think of, in this case:

To me.

At the library.

Take time to consider both possibilities and weigh them on the scale of better or worse.

Spend a few quiet hours in the woods listening to the heart speak and whether or not it agreed with the assessment of his mind.

Say yes out loud. Say no likewise. And feel how each answer rings inside once all possible information is present.

By the time he returned, covered in sweat, the sun had dropped behind the horizon depositing a light show worthy of the tropics: aqua, coral, blush, and pineapple gold melding like sheer pigment on silk.

He joined me on the porch after a cool shower where I sat with a stray cat who befriended us on a sub-zero night the previous January. We named him Miles and ushered him in on freezing nights. My father kept a pile of old blankets near the door until spring. Miles jumped down from my legs and up onto the white wooden balustrade that extended our apartment when summer days sizzled well into the dark.

Between us, my father arranged two glasses of lemonade and a small glass plate of ginger cookies shaped like windmills—two for me and one for him. He'd forgone a second cookie to minimize a little of the belly fat that started collecting when he switched to less strenuous work. Whether that actually worked or not decidedly remained his business.

"Well, Son. I'm coming with you."

"That's great! What made you decide?"

"I figured out a long time ago that being loved is a good thing and so is having the opportunity to love. But I have a couple of non-negotiable items that we need to discuss." He sipped his drink.

"Alright."

"Good. Okay, Son. We can't share a household anymore. You should find an apartment or your own house, and I'll do the same."

"I think that's a good idea. I may find a good lady and living with you might cramp my style."

My father laughed.

"Anything else, Dad?"

"We have a standing dinner together once a week only. I hate to be so standard, Son, but I would like it to be on Sundays at my place. No dropping in and raiding each other's refrigerators at all hours of the day or night and, the good Lord forbid, a weekday."

I laughed. "Agreed. What else?"

"The rest we'll make up as we go, but know the lines of communication are always open."

"I accept all three demands."

My father raised his eyebrows and chuckled at the word "demands," pleased for some reason. He stood to his feet and offered his hand. "Then Green Mountain here we come." And we shook.

I shook my father's hand in an entirely new way.

MY FATHER'S PERMANENTLY scarred skin wrapped his face's bony structure with little give. It refused to grow hair anymore. We never once discussed what happened. And as much as I wanted to know how badly it hurt and how long it took to heal, his longstanding silence on the matter told me he deserved to bear this part of him without question from anybody. Even his son.

I didn't press him.

I wondered if my father's wisdom taught me that, or if my love for him, nurtured by him so thoroughly in the deepest hollows of my heart, grew to instinctively know what he required of me.

I do remember this, though.

"Everybody has a right to share what they want about themselves. Being curious is fine, but trust me, Son, if you can feel a shift in the conversation when defensiveness begins, that's your signal to just go ahead and stop talking."

50

M Y FATHER LOCATED a modest, single-story house for rent on Garner Street with two bedrooms and a bath. "The yard will be nice for Miles," he said casually, as if I knew all along he'd take the cat. Which I did. A shed out back to store his statues and carvings as well as a push mower and garden tools was definitely a plus. But, in the detached garage, a workbench had already been installed. "That right there," he whispered, pointing his finger. "I'm sold."

Inside, light green walls and freshly sanded, polished oak floors set his mind to homemaking and he walked right to the furniture store on Second Street. He bought himself a double bed, a new chest of drawers, a sofa, a reclining easy chair, and a coffee table. He kept the old dinette because, as he put it, "Who wouldn't want a table with birds and flowers on it?"

Six blocks away, at the other end of town, an apartment

on the upper floor of a foursquare became my first abode. Thinking I rented it because it reminded me of home would be a bad assumption. The only other dwelling for rent bore my father's new address.

My father gave me almost all of the old furniture. "This might just be the last chance I have to pick out what I'd like. I never have before. So, pick out what you want, and we'll get rid of the rest before the movers come."

A perfect arrangement.

I set up my old bed in the front bedroom with a new mattress, bedsheets, and a bedspread any grandmother would have happily slipped in-between. In the back bedroom, I placed the old sofa where I could read and watch television, as well as my old desk and lamp where I could write up reports in the evening. For a housewarming gift, my father purchased a new dinette with steel tubing for legs—and not a bird in sight.

Two days after we arrived, he had already finished decorating his home across town with a few sculptures, photographs, and paintings I had never before viewed.

"Just old college stuff," he said.

"You did those?"

"A long time ago."

Sheer curtains from McFarland's Variety, blue throw pillows, and a yellow rug—once Keziah's—dressed up the living room where Miles decided to eternally roost on the back of the new white sofa.

"Are you going to purchase some new living room furniture, Son?" he asked at our first Sunday Dinner of roast beef, mashed potatoes, and string beans.

"I'll probably just go ahead and let the lady do it."

"You mean your landlord? Doesn't she already have furniture of her own?" He winked. My father had never winked at me before that moment. Winks like that are powerful stuff.

Apparently, my father was a prophet.

51

AT SEVENTEEN I asked my father, "Dad, what is salvation?"

"Knowing who you really are."

"And who's that?"

"I can't tell you that any more than you can tell me, Son. But I will tell you this. It's a discovery like no other once you're given the answer."

52

ROUTINE SETTLED IN more quickly than expected. Late summer bowed to an autumn subsequently pushed away by a deep snowfall at November's middle. After Christmas, winter set in more firmly than the hairdo of the widow who made an appointment at least once a week. She ran the funeral home and, in her defense, possessed real issues, in spite of the fact she knew more ways a human being could die than any doctor I have ever known. And if a doctor could keep up with her, I doubt he'd rate them on Mrs. Blake's revolving one to ten scale.

"That one was a solid seven on the scale of gruesome."

"Mr. Jimmy was a ten. Everyone wants that on the scale of easy."

I assumed he passed in his sleep after a long life of bacon, eggs, and Parliaments.

I never minded seeing her, and if a patient materialized with such regularity, having one that laughed at herself, loved people, and stood firm in the face of death gave me nothing to complain about.

I'd battened down the clinic for the night and the following day, Sunday. The need presented in Green Mountain proved so great even working six days a week couldn't keep me ahead. My father and I had been invited to dine at my landlord's house, the first social engagement I had ever accepted with my father.

Christmastime was mostly stored in attics by that point, only a few decorations straggled in the front windows of the Main Street storefronts run by less than persnickety merchants.

Bundled up in our overcoats, scarves, and hats, the wind just shy of bitter, we held the fruits of our errand, a box of chocolates held by my father, a bouquet of hothouse roses in my grip.

"Do you know who you really are, Dad?" I asked him a block away from home.

"I do now."

"When did you realize it?"

"I'm not exactly sure, Son. But I can tell you this. It happened step-by-step along the way."

The small appliance repair place sparkled almost apologetically with beleaguered garland and holly ready to flare up at even an unkind word or two. We waved to LeRoy Price, the owner, a man who had lost his son in Poland three days before the war ended in Europe. He waved back.

"Can you sum up who you are, Dad? Do you even want to?"

"That's easy, Son. Love."

All of our previous conversations readied me for his occasional obscurity, but apparently not quite to this extent. Every once in a great while, I confess, I had to wonder about my father.

"You're love."

"Yes, I am."

"I'm not sure how a human being can just be love, Dad. How do you know?"

"Because every time I say or do or think something that's not, I feel like I just descended into a hell of my own making."

"I get that."

We continued the walk to my apartment house where I wanted to clean up a bit before dinner. The people of the town who saw us waved. Some called out a greeting and we replied in kind.

"I thought we'd be met with more suspicion." I let us into my door.

"Look at us, Son. We have that overall air of, 'Haven't they been through enough already?' don't we?"

I laughed. "Yes, we do."

"And they know you're here to help. They're not stupid."

"And they know you're the one who raised me that way."

My father took off his hat and laid it on the kitchen counter. "That's a very magnanimous thought, Son. But you decided to step out in life and I'm proud of you for that. Among other things." He grinned.

"Like what?" I asked freely, without fear.

He didn't take the opportunity to check my ego, for he had told me years before the world did that job effortlessly. No. He would offer something altogether different than what society served. Unconditional love seemed a little foolish-seeming when viewed without context, he once told me. But if he had even the smallest chance to give that to someone while he lived on Earth, I was certainly his best bet.

As I washed my face, brushed my teeth, and polished up my hand, he told me all the good he saw in me. He even thanked me for the opportunity. "You know, Son, you could have been much harder to raise."

"Maybe you raised me to not be so hard."

"Well, that right there is a chicken and an egg and we've done away with that."

I let him get away with it.

But I felt his words ringing inside of me. I would have bet the entire wad in J.P. Morgan's pocket when we went down for dinner at Della May's I was a good man for all a young widow needed, for she resided in a world where husbands can be shot down over Scandinavia leaving wives with a baby girl.

A world she learned to navigate on her own.

Three weeks later, after our first kiss, Della May whispered, "I don't need you to save me, Taliesin. I want the love of a kind human being and a compassionate soul. Nothing else accepted."

"Why is that?" I asked.

"My daughter deserves no less, and the same goes for me."

I was definitely the man for the job.

53

Della May deigned to marry me nine months later. We set the adoption process in motion for Martha as soon as we arrived home from our honeymoon. We lazed for two weeks at the seashore cottage Della May had dreamed about since she was a little girl. Two weeks of lavish food and sunrises over the beach, sunsets behind the sound, and, "No prosthesis in bed, Tally. I just want you."

At the courthouse on a spring day while cherry trees shed their petals along the walk, I became a father, and knowing all that might, could, and did entail, I prayed to be the man for the job. If not, John would never be to blame.

My father became "Granddaddy."

And Della May shone like the sun, and I the moon reflected in her beautiful, golden light.

Martha jumped into my arms and kissed me hard on each cheek. "Mmm! You're *my* Daddy now! And that is *that*." She wriggled down and hugged my father's legs.

"And you're my Granddaddy, Granddaddy."

"Yes, I am. And it's quite the honor, Martha."

"Call me Mart, Granddaddy."

He looked at Della May, then at me, then at Martha. "There don't seem to be any objections, so Mart it is, Mart."

There were stars all over the place that day.

NINE YEARS OLD, Martha already spoke her mind and viewed the world through the perception her travels in it had allowed and manufactured so far. Della May, loving and kind, resembled my father in many ways, only to the accompaniment of her own singing. But parenthood came upon me if not full-grown, then definitely preparing for puberty.

"There are some days I just don't know what to do, Dad."

"Son, there are some days you just don't."

He'd arrived at the clinic needing a few stitches, something that happened every three months or so now. Either his fine motor skills were going, his eyesight, or his focus. But so far, he left every morning for the local carpenter, and Lester wasn't complaining.

"What did you do with me on days like that?"

"I just did what I knew," he said, watching as I

numbed his thumb.

"What was that?"

"Distract and converse."

"Ah."

"Like you're doing right now."

The light dawned suddenly on all the times I'd come home from school with a problem, or when I berated myself for my inability to complete a newly required task with ease, and all the times I began to hate myself for things I couldn't help. Even when the principal suspended me from school, three times to be exact, and every single one of them for punching the sneaky class bully who always took me past my limit without an audience, I was proclaimed the violent one. In some ways, I guess I was. It doesn't help to pretend a punch is a caress, because it just isn't. After each incident, my father took the day off and played board games with me during my exile. "Every man has his limit, Son."

It appeared my father's distractions were commensurate to his lack of a plan and how much time it would take to come up with one, from an ice cream cone, to a walk in the woods, to a train-to-train trip when a young man might settle for less because he couldn't imagine something more.

"Mostly, you worked things out in those spaces on your own. I just told you what I knew and let you incorporate that into your own situation, Son. Because the truth is, I'm not you. I could only help you see the power of your own free will."

"'And what a privilege and honor it is to have one,'" I quoted his words.

I clipped the stitching and bandaged his wound.

"Thank you, Son. That was a fine job."

"It took a lot of chickens, Dad."

And we laughed as he slid off the table. "I'll see you at three on Sunday?"

"We'll be there. What are you making?"

"Chicken."

"Did you just decide that?"

My father shrugged into his jacket. "Well, Son, let's just keep that a mystery between us."

"I'll see you Sunday."

55

MY FATHER ARRIVED at our home at three o'clock on a dark morning, a belching sleet quickly covering the roads. Della May's labor set on at two-thirty, the hospital an hour away on clear roads. I had delivered one baby in my residency at University Hospital and had hoped to never again repeat the experience, particularly on my own wife. Thankfully, each contraction waited ten minutes after its predecessor to arrive. And in her own words, "Martha didn't want to leave the confines, so I imagine this one will be no different."

"Is Mart still asleep?" my father asked as he slipped off his rubber overshoes and set them to dry on the braided rug near the coat rack flanking the back door.

"She is." Della May sauntered into the kitchen completely at ease, considering. My, but that woman was just as beautiful pregnant as not. "We thought it best to go on ahead and let her get the full night in." She kissed my father on the cheek. "Thank you, Granddaddy."

"Aw, I'm happy to help, Dell. You two get on now."

My father did his best to remain calm and affable, his gift to us in our joy. The last time somebody labored nearby, two people eventually died, one he would never hold, the other he would never hold again.

"Alright, then!" I clapped him on the back. "We're off!"

"Coffee's in the percolator already," Della May said. "All for you, Daddy!"

My father laughed. To the rest of the world, it would have sounded like any laugh, but being my father, I knew better.

Normally I would have let him think he fooled me, but I was his son and I had become a man. "It's going to be alright, Dad. I can promise you that."

And I embraced my father.

"Go on now," he said, again, cheerfully, and pulled away.

"You, alright?"

"Yes. Yes I am, Son." He had changed back in an instant.

I asked him about it a few years later and my father told me he knew that night whatever life handed me, I could handle it, not because I would always *find* a way, but because I had become the way itself.

My father had revealed it day by day, what that looked like, what it sounded like, and most importantly, what it felt like.

The point was, I knew.

56

WHEN I HANDED my father five-day-old Janet, he wept the holiest tears I'd ever witnessed.

And when he kissed my daughter and said, "Mart, come keep Granddaddy company while I get acquainted with your baby sister," I wept some of my own. Della May did, too.

I STITCHED UP my father with greater frequency. Finally, the week before Janet's fifth Christmas I said, "Permission to speak as your physician, Dad."

"Go right ahead, Doctor," he said, completely serious.

I'd never felt so proud of who I had become before or since.

"Your injuries are becoming deeper and much too frequent. Do you have any inkling why?"

He held out his hands and reached forward. When his arms lengthened, both hands trembled. "How long have you been experiencing tremors?"

"Years. So—Doctor."

"How did I not notice this?"

"Happened only when I reached out and strained a bit, but now ..."

"Benign Tremor Syndrome," I said.

"Is that so? I have to admit I've been hiding it from

you your whole life."

"Why, Dad?"

I was his son again.

"At first I didn't want to ever give you anything to worry about. You'd already lost your mother so you deserved to be certain about your father. I kept my reach in as much as possible, and as it never seemed to get worse, I didn't worry, really. And then, when you lost a hand, well, how could my little issue compare? There always seemed a good reason to keep it under wraps."

"What do you think is happening to you now? Are you reaching out more in your work?"

"That might explain it."

"Why?"

"I can't carve anymore, Son. My eyesight has gotten too poor. Lester's just got me planing and cutting, and I have to extend my reach sometimes and it's all pretty clumsy. Honestly, I'm not exactly sure why he doesn't fire me."

I could have told him that. Who wouldn't want my father around?

"Dad, I need to ask you a favor."

"What do you need, Son?"

"I'm almost forty years old now. I need you to start telling me when something is wrong."

"But Son, that's—"

"No, Dad. The game has changed. Knowledge isn't a thing to be avoided to save me from grief. It's needed now to ward off unnecessary decline and injury as long as possible. Please tell me you can understand that."

My father sat for half a minute then spoke. "I can see

the wisdom of that. But Son, in light of that, I have my own request to make."

"Please go ahead."

"I'm seventy years old and I have lived a life I am good and proud of. I mastered a craft and I loved you the best way I knew how. As my doctor and my son, please respect what I have to say."

"Go ahead, Dad."

"I want to leave this planet the way I came, letting nature take its course whenever, wherever, and whatever that may be. Now"—he held up a scarred hand—"I don't mean I don't want to be made comfortable. But I want my time left on Earth to be just what it's always been."

"And what is that?"

"The simple opportunity to just be alive and happy about it."

"And 'when it's time to go home, go home as quickly and safely as possible,'" I quoted.

"Yes, Son," he said. "That about sums it up."

58

And that is exactly what happened. At the age of eighty-two, having loved Della May, Martha, Janet, our newest addition, James, and me to the best of his ability, my father suffered a stroke that left him paralyzed on his right side. He moved in and somehow maintained his joy for the next two years. Miles relocated his roost to the lounge chair, right by my father's head.

My father never faltered, even when he lost control of his body. He presented himself to us not in what he could do no longer, but having come to be exactly what he wanted and who—simply being. And he loved every single one of us merely by looking at us, sitting with us, raising the left side of his mouth in a smile. We all knew, when we sat with my father we sat in the bright and powerful presence of unconditional love, and the troubadour of beauty found a new way to carve her path in our hearts. Our final words to one another told the entire tale as we somehow knew it would.

"I love you, Son." The words would have been unintelligible had I not heard them every day of my life.

"I love you, Dad."

He left us within the hour.

I suppose some might suspect my father too good to be true, and I wouldn't blame them. But I believe we live in a universe of infinite possibilities. In that universe rests the possibility of a perfect father, and he was mine.

Rest in Peace, Dad.

Rest in Love.

And thank you for all the ways I have become the love you gave.

I see. I know. And I am very truly,

Your Son,

    Taliesin

THE END

ACKNOWLEDGMENTS

Many thanks to Len Sweet for extending the license to write about the love of God in metaphor and for making it possible on so many fronts. To The Salish Sea Press team: Len, Carmen, Joanna, Lynn, Melissa, and Adam, I appreciate you all so much in everything you've done to bring this book to light. So much love and gratitude to my children: Ty, Jake, Gwynnie, and Matt for all you are and continue to be. To all of my family, friends, and readers who have supported my creative endeavors for so long, I am grateful. May God bless you all.

About the Author

Lisa Samson writes about life, what it is, and how it can be if we live in love.

She has authored more than forty books and is a twice recipient of Christianity Today's Novel of the Year as well as a three-time winner of The Christy Award.

Lisa lives on a farm in Tennessee and loves her children, nature, and anything to do with outer space.

Connect with Lisa:
Website: https://lisajoysamson.com
Facebook: https://www.facebook.com/writerlisasamson
Instagram: @lisajoysamson
The Salish Sea Press: https://Salishsea.press

Other Titles by Lisa

The Church Ladies

The Passion of Mary-Margaret

The Living End

Tiger Lillie

Resurrection in May

Straight Up

Club Sandwich

Books Written With Leonard Sweet

St.Is

Songs of Light

Made in the USA
Coppell, TX
12 June 2021